A SUSURI

OF

GHOSTS

RICK

LEE

somehow came here from a small town further south called Saltburn-by-the-Sea.

Last is the hound, a very faint creature, who is the least scary, probably because she wasn't scary when she was alive. Anna was a kind gentle person, who lived in a lovely cottage further north, where the three of them had reappeared when those bad people kidnapped that girl . . . which I can't explain . . . can ghosts really travel to different places? It seems they can!

But now they've been joined recently by another – a glittery kingfisher, who was a sad lady called Freya, who had the most amazing memory. Just one read of a document then she could recall it word for word. This, of course, made her a treasure for various organisations and a target for their enemies. Ex-DS Janet Becket was once appointed her bodyguard and they were sent to an isolated house up in the mountains. But given that was Becket, she wouldn't tell you much about it.

And why are they all here?

A house we'd started living in when it was Covid.

By 'we', I mean now just me, Janet and Ziggy.

Ah, Ziggy, Sigismund Hook, computer whizz and interferer in all things mysterious, who constantly gets us all involved in terrible political and violent activities.

The other folk around here you'll meet eventually. They're not ghosts, but they're becoming a sort of gang of interfering busybodies, who are also constantly getting into all sorts of trouble.

The last 'adventure' we all ended up in the middle of France, even me for heaven's sake, trying to rescue a girl called Maria, who some people, some very dangerous people, thought she was a descendant of one of the Romanoff family, which of course didn't go down well with the Russians. Anyway, it was all hushed up and we were all spoken to severely by scary government people who Ziggy calls 'men in black'.

I don't know what happened to the girl . . . or her mother.

Anyway, that's all over now.

But don't relax.
I'm sure there will be more trouble coming our way.
Ziggy's constantly monitoring what's going on.

What I have heard is that DI Magda Steil has decided to retire, although she can't be more than forty something and her brother, Tomasz, has promised his mother, Helena, not to get into any more trouble, which no-one believes for one second. As far as I know he's still shadowed by a weird woman called Imelda, who's covered in scary tattoos . . . no surname I've ever heard. They all live in a huge house high up above us on the sunny side of the valley.

I don't know yet whether this means that the stand-in couple, who covered for Magda, after she had that dreadful fall from her horse, will return from Edinburgh. As odd a couple you're likely to meet. DI Walker is black and his sidekick DS Gill who is an expert in some kind of karate.

To be honest I think these last few weeks have been the longest period of time when we've not been embroiled in all sorts of life and death struggle.

'Something to do with the river,' mutters Ziggy.

'So, what's so special about the Tweed,' I ask, innocently, which just makes him roll his eyes . . . and given today's makeup, that's not what you want to see as darkness falls.

Oh, I nearly forgot . . . me and Janet . . . we're . . . er . . . lovers?

I know . . . I still can't believe it!

*   *   *

'Well, things could be worse,' murmurs Gill.

This only gets a hard stare in the mirror from Walker who's driving.

She shrugs and checks her phone.

Nothing.

She looks out the window.

The standard Borders sky. Grey clouds in a grey sky above leafless trees and drab houses.

They just drove over a bridge with a river in spate heavily lumbering along.

She sighs . . . her thoughts going to the big hills of her childhood.

On impulse she dabs her friend's number.

She's about to give up when a soft voice answers . . . in Gaelic which makes her smile, so she responds in the same language.

Walker frowns and then has to listen to words softly spoken which have no meaning to him.

So there's a few smiles and then a laugh, but then Gill's just listening, only murmuring a few words . . . until the call finishes.

He glances across at her. Her face often doesn't tell him what she's thinking, but this doesn't look good.

'Okay?' he ventures.

No response.

He knows better than to push. Particularly with her.

But then he sees a café, surprisingly open on a day like this.

He pulls over, parks and waits.

Nothing. Her eyes looking straight ahead, but obviously not seeing what's there. He mutters about wanting a coffee. No response. He decides to leave her and quielty gets out of the car.

He's got his coffee and a biscuit and found a place to look out at the grey hills before she appears.

She sits down but looks away.

'Coffee?' he murmurs.

She shrugs.

He decides that's the nearest to a 'yes' he's going to get, so goes off to get one, returns with some chocolate bars as well.

And then he waits.

He guesses it's a good five minutes before she reaches for the cup and takes a few sips.

'Have you got any sisters . . . or brothers?' she asks without looking at him.

He frowns, his head immediately filled with the mayhem of his childhood.

'Uhuh, three older sisters and a younger brother.'

This makes her frown and glance at him.

'Really?'

'Fraid so,' he laughs, 'didn't get a word in ever, just told what to do and knew I had to.'

This only gets a small shrug.

But then nothing.

He waits.

'I wasn't there when my mother died . . . I was in Afghanistan,' she whispers.

He can't think of any response to that.

'It took three days to contact me and then another week before I got home.'

Again silence seemed the only option.

'My father never forget me . . . drinking himself to death.'

All sorts of scenarios running around in his head, but he waits, assuming the worst.

She shrugs.

'I'll have to go,' she says, now looking at him.

He waits again, resisting the temptation to put his hand on hers.

'The neighbours found him up on the hillside, in the little lochan where he used to fish.'

Now he did reach out to her . . . and she let him.

*   *   *

Imelda doesn't get many calls and she sometimes forgets where she's left her old mobile. This doesn't bother someone who would prefer to forget a lot of her past and the bad people she used to know.

But this one is intriguing because she recognises the number. A number she had assumed was long deleted.

So she hesitates, wondering who it might be. The woman it belonged to died three or four years ago. An artist who befriended her when she was still going back to see her father.

She glances behind her.

She's out on the terrace, but she can hear Tomasz and his mother laughing about something.

So she presses the button.

'Hello,' says a voice.

Imelda is more puzzled, that's not a Scottish accent. American?

'Hello,' she mutters, 'who are you?'

There's a pause.

'Ah . . . that's a bit difficult . . . I think you knew my mother?'

Imelda frowned . . . and waits.

'On Harris . . . she was an artist.'

Again Imelda is puzzled, thinking Jean never mentioned any children . . . or a husband for that matter.

'You mean Jean?' she murmurs, thinking this is more than strange.

'Ah, well, that was why it took me a long time to find her. That wasn't her real name. She was called Pauline. Pauline Guest.'

Imelda can't think whether she ever said her surname and her paintings were always signed JS.

There's another awkward pause.

'I don't suppose she told you about me?'

This sounded angry, so Imelda hesitated.

'She left my father when I was sixteen, he spent a lot of time and money trying to find her, but . . . it wasn't until after he'd died that I found the files on his laptop. Emails and a list of addresses of all the people he contacted.'

Imelda waits, thinking this is a bit creepy. Why does this keep happening to her? She thinks she'll just stop the call.

'Don't end the call . . . please,' says the woman.

Imelda waits.

Is the woman crying?

No, it's the rustling of papers.

She realises Tomasz and Helena have stopped talking and turns to see him standing at the doorway, a frown on his face.

'The thing is,' the woman continues, 'I've also found I had a brother, but can't find anything about him apart from a birth certificate . . . if he is alive he'd be twenty-five.'

Tomasz has now come down the steps and is standing beside her giving her a quizzical look.

Imelda shakes her head at him. He backs off and goes to sit on the balustrade.

She tunes back into the woman, who's saying 'meet up . . . please?'

Imelda hesitates, but in the end her curiosity is stronger than her fear.

The call finished she shakes her head at Tomasz who comes to stand with her, realises she's crying and puts his arms around her.

Later when she's told him what the woman had said, he agrees to accompany her to the hotel where the woman is staying.

*   *   *

There are hundreds of big houses in the Borders, some of them dating back to the eleventh century and beyond. Some of them are now hotels, but a lot of them are still in the hands of the families who've lived there for generations.

They've been involved in the numerous wars and Borders raiding, changing sides being a frequent option taken, so they know about security and keeping safe.

This also included taking care of the numerous pots and pans and trinkets, which have been for ever accruing more value and the expense of keeping them safe.

The older houses were built to make sure the raiders couldn't easily get access and many have priest holes and cellars and secret doors and false walls to keep themselves and their treasures hidden. This also means there's a few firms around who specialise in expensive equipment and systems to protect them from more sophisticated burglars.

And the big house just a few miles up hill from Jedburgh is a fine example of this. The drive is nearly half a mile long winding through the forest of firs and oaks and beech trees. This time of year the firs are the only ones left with greenery, but at night you'd soon be lost if you strayed from the main drive. Especially as the lights that normally light the winding road are turned off while the family are not in residence.

They'd been there for Hogmanay, of course, as well as the thirty or more guests for the eight days of jollification and the murdering of hundreds of birds bred specifically for this annual slaughter. But now the forest lies silent as the family and all their guests have flown off to better climes or back to the business of making more money as if they really needed it.

So the few creatures who don't go to sleep in the winter are gradually recovering their dark and lonely paradise now all the cleaners have gone as well. The crows welcoming the dawn and then a few hours later swarming before an early roost. The surviving deer and grouse picking at the ground and rooting out what they can.

But above all the silence.

So who are these folk?
Three figures softly stalking through the trees.
Each of them carrying something, as well as a rucksack.
Two of them have ropes coiled across their chests.
The smaller one has what looks like a cross bow.
They're not speaking but seem to know exactly where they're going.

If the owners could see them now, the first question would be 'how did they get this far?' What's happened to the alarms on the gates and the tripwires in the woods?

They stop where the trees give way to the lawns. Although eventually some local hired hand will come to mow them, but that's a couple of months away. Everything was mowed and cut back before the celebrations.

Their clothing is dark and it's difficult to make out their gender, as they're all wearing balaclavas. Instead of carrying on across the lawn, the smallest one retrieves some metal devices from a rucksack.

The small one then attaches them to his/her legs and then uses these devices to climb a huge fir tree.

Within only a few minutes the dark figure has clambered thirty or forty feet up in the darkness.

The other two watch and wait.

There's a swishing sound and a metallic thud high up on the wall.

The shadow above them then appears to fly through the air and lands like a monkey on the edge of a second-floor window.

Silence.

Punctured by a high-pitched whine, which only lasts a few seconds and then the figure can be seen pushing the window open and climbing inside.

The two waiting don't move.

It's only a few moments before a rope comes flying down.

The two waiting cross the lawn and the path and quickly ascend. First the tall one and then the heavier one.

Silence.

Maybe half an hour . . . forty minutes . . . no longer, and they reappear one after the other abseiling quickly down. The small one coming last after a couple of minutes delay and quickly retrieves the rope.

No words are spoken as they slip through the trees, climb over the wall and back to the old landrover parked by the wall.

The only difference from the outside being the plastic cover taped to the hole in the glass in the window on the second floor . . . which no one realises is there until a fortnight later when the caretaker makes a cursory tour of the house. Even then he wouldn't have spotted it unless he wondered why the room was so cold.

He calls the family and eventually they comprehend they've been robbed.

There are plenty of other expensive items in the house, but the safe held the most treasured possessions handed down for hundreds of years from the time when the border was a fluctuating ragged line across the hills.

A necklace of rubies given to the Countess by Mary Queen of Scots.

Two beautiful glass bowls from Elizabeth the First.

Other priceless relics of the family's wavering loyalties.

Other trinkets and baubles that had been stashed away and rarely shown and never in public.

Hundreds of years of nightmares that they might be discovered.

*   *   *

'Sir Richard Lee.'

'Who?'

Ex Di Fletcher is standing behind his 'granddaughter', Eleanora 'Ellie' Camville, looking at what seems gibberish to him, another ancient document with spidery black handwriting . . . although for once it's not in Latin as he spots the word 'walls'.

She turns to look up at him.

The vivid green eyes as scary as ever.

'Fifteen fifties he was sent to review and then rebuild the walls at Berwick.'

Fletcher can't think whether he's been there or not, but that's not surprising, she has a habit of taking him to places he's never even heard of before, although in this case he has heard the name.

'So . . .'

'Someone a bit like you . . .' she murmurs.

He frowns.

'How do you mean?' he demands, thinking the worst.

'Difficult, argumentative, secretive – given to cutting corners.'

Fletcher is only mildly troubled by this but can't help but laugh.

'How so?' he grumbles.

'Also someone who got sent to all sorts of different places and had arguments and altercations with lots of people.'

Again he can't deny that.

There's a pause as she shuffles some of her papers. She knows this isn't how most students work now, everything on their laptop, but she likes the physical presence of the scraps of her notes, often in her own shorthand, which would take some translation.

'And given the times he lived in he was adept at surviving – not losing his head . . . literally.'

'When was this?' he asks, genuinely interested.

'The worst time to be alive and religious,' she mutters, 'and he certainly wasn't.'

As someone who has seen a myriad dead bodies and met some very evil people, he'd long lost any belief in any such being as a god.

But she was continuing the lecture.

' . . . after Henry the Eighth broke with Rome, his son Edward was a waste of space who dithered for the few years he was king, his elder sister Mary wasn't called Bloody for nothing, killing thousands of protestants and then Elizabeth, who it must be said only believed in one thing – her own survival, whatever that required.'

Fletcher has seen his 'not granddaughter' angry before, but he could only just stand mouth open at this outburst.

She turns to look at him, her eyes blazing . . . but then bursts out laughing.

'My, my,' comes a voice from behind him.

He doesn't need to look.

Louisa Cunninghame 'sashays' past him as only she can 'sashay'.

'Methinks the lady doth protest too much.'

'Well,' says Ellie, 'she wasn't the worst murderer in the Scottish Borders, hundreds of others who could make that claim.'

'But she did get the walls done,' said Louisa.

'Ah, well, as ever with her, they were never finished, she never paid her debts.'

'Well they look pretty good to me, they're still there. I doubt much of what's built nowadays will be standing in five hundred years' time.'

Ellie shrugs.

'So Berwick?' says Fletcher, 'I don't think you've ever taken me there?'

'Well, then, we shall go!' cries Ellie, leaping up.

This, of course, means the creature lying by her feet throughout this conversation now also comes to life – furiously going round and round in circles at the possibility of a walk – or a run in his case.

'Come on Rollo, let's go!'

*   *   *

Historically there have been many people and events in the Scottish Borders which include caves in their stories. The most famous ones 'belong' to St Cuthbert whose walk goes from Melrose to Lindisfarne, but there other less well-known ones.

So very few people know of the one hidden high up in a cliff not that far from Norham castle.

Even in the height of late summer it's still damp and would give you a chill if you were unwise enough to spend a night there.

But the creature which inhabits it has long forgotten how long he's been there.

A cave.

Thirty feet up from the river, which crashes its way through the remains of the igneous dyke which provoked the sharp change in direction.

Rarely visited.

The last being a man entangled in the remains of a broken rope ladder impaled on one of the metal struts fixed here hundreds of years ago.

That body was retrieved.

But the older occupying spirit was awakened by the clambering rescue team.

A ghostly presence already long confused in its own memories.

The cave is cold.

The voice is masked by the sound of the river.

But occasionally a mouse or a bird momentarily creeps inside and then realises there's already an occupant.

Whispering and moaning to itself.

It had a name once.
But long forgotten.
It had fine clothes back then.
But now they're dust and tattered scraps.

But the sense of the betrayal still lingers.

And the memory of the evil monster who betrayed him still enough to cause a howl of anger.

CHAPTER TWO

Walker and DS Gatti are standing outside the gates of the big house, although they can't actually see it as the trees block the view.

They've been waiting for nearly half an hour and Walker's thinking of climbing over. He knows Gill would have been over twenty minutes ago, but she's still up north, no messages received.

'What do you know?' he asks Gatti.

The sergeant shrugs and shakes his head.

'They're very rich . . . but don't live here all the time . . . other houses in the UK and elsewhere.'

Walker shakes his head.

'So they only come here for the parties and the grouse shooting?'

Gatti sighs and looks away, there's nothing he can do or say about that. He knows it's just as bad in Tuscany where he comes from, which gives him a pang of homesickness.

Walker turns to look at the gates again.

'There was a time I'd be over these gates and . . .'

But Gatti looks down the lane thinking he can hear a vehicle coming.

It turns up five minutes later. An old Land Rover carrying an older man, who takes his time getting out of the vehicle, although his two dogs in the back are not so slow. They both do a turn around the two officers and, deciding they're not any danger, give the nearest walls and trees some watering.

Andrew Jardine takes out a handful of keys from his pocket without saying a word, chooses the big one and goes to the gate.

Five minutes later they're standing outside the main door which is a good ten steps up from the drive.

Jardine stands jangling the keys and gives a sigh.

'Do you want to go inside first or have a look at where they got in?'

Walker shrugs.

'Let's see point of entry first I think.'

So they follow the old man round the corner and another twenty yards or so, until he stops and points up at one of the second-floor windows.

Walker stares up at it then takes a few steps back.

The walls are made of huge chunks of stone but it would be hard to climb and there aren't any nearby drainpipes.

'We've nae ladder high enough fer that,' mutters Jardine. 'I think ye might be looking for the fire brigade.'

Walker can't disagree with him and then looks at the nearest fir trees, which are a good cricket pitch length away and in any case they're not much higher than the windows. So . . .

They follow the old man back to the main door.

It takes three keys to open, including the huge one which is probably as old as the house.

Inside it's the grandeur Walker's come to expect from the Borders rich.

Lots of huge paintings of forbears he assumes, many of them in kilts and plaid jackets. The few ladies in huge dresses and ridiculous hats. Many of them accompanied by the corpses of deer and other dead creatures.

They follow the old man up to the second floor and he shows them into the small room which has the safe in the wall, although probably normally hidden behind the painting which is leaning on the floor beneath it.

Walker looks around.

No damage he can see apart from the hole in the window, still covered by a piece of plastic. Even though the safe in the wall is open there are no other signs of entry or exit.

He goes to the window and pulls it open. Nothing on the inside or the outside ledges.

'So there's no alarm in this room?'

'Aye that's reet,' growls the old man. 'They are too tight fisted to put alarms up here . . . although I think the safe itself has an alarm fitted and you'd have to know the numbers to open it.'

Walker nods at him and turns to Gatti.

He shrugs.

'They've not contacted us about safety precautions, but then the rich folk don't tend to do that anyway.'

Walker looks away.

In his heart he knows he can't be bothered. They'll be covered by insurance and won't feel the pinch.

He goes again to look out the window.

He pulls himself up to look down at the outside.

There are a few chunks of mortar missing, but nothing to indicate someone scrabbling up or through the window.

Even though he's only sticking his head out it makes him dizzy looking down, so he retreats.

He looks at Gatti, who shakes his head.

'Not me sir, I get dizzy standing on a stepladder, I couldn't look out that window never mind climb out of it.'

Walker shrugs.

But now they can hear the investigating team arriving, jeeps and vans scrunching up the drive.

He waits until the team leader arrives, already in his white overalls.

Why are these guys so annoyingly happy in their job, he wonders?

SOCO team leader Frank Simpson scans the room.

'I do like a tidy crew,' he mutters. 'Most criminals are so untidy they generally leave something, but . . . this looks really clean.'

Walker shakes his head.

'Come and look out here,' he says and takes him across to the window.

'I can't see how they got in?'

Simpson pokes his head out.

'Yeh, I see what you mean. We'll need the fire brigade I think,' which makes the old man wink at him.

So Walker decides to get out of their way and beckons Gatti to follow him back downstairs and round to the outside again. To confirm to himself he paces out the distance from the nearest tree to the wall and finds he was a couple of yards short – a good twenty-four yards.

He goes to look at the trunk of the tree.

He's no expert on trees, so as far he's concerned it's a fir tree, although he knows there are different types. He gives Gatti an inquisitive glance. He shrugs and murmurs 'Douglas fir? Maybe?'

Walker shakes his head.

'Where's the gillie's daughter when you need her,' he grumbles.

'Afternoon, sir,' says a voice. 'Yer not taking up tree hugging are you? I wouldn't advise a Scots pine, they're a bit tae 'joozy'.'

He turns round to see DS Gill, in her green stalker's coat.

'Where did they get in?' she asks, looking up.

He shrugs and points up at the window.

Gill goes up to the wall and scratches at the pointing without making much effect.

She looks up at the window again.

'You'd need a terrific head for heights and I doubt I'd feel safe on that wall.'

Then she walks away to look up at the distance between the trees and the wall.

'We need the fire brigade.'

She turns to find Walker pointing at his phone as he waits for an answer.

Call finished he nods.

'They're on their way.'

*   *   *

The Borders' gossip network – well, the older, richer one – quickly informs Magda about the break-in, even though it makes her sigh. It may be efficient but the assumption is that even if one of your daughters abnormally takes up a job with the polis, she is still one of them – as also the honour eventually bestowed on the Polish lady, her mother, who her father strangely retrieved from behind the Iron Curtain.

So later she tells Tomasz, who just shrugs, he's no time for the man who'd married into an old Border's family, which was becoming a bit of a pattern . . . he's no time for most Americans, particularly after meeting quite a few in Afghanistan – "arrogant and ignorant' were the best words to describe most of them.

'What did they take?' he asks.

Magda frowns and then laughs.

'You don't think they told the police, do you?'

Tomasz smiles.

'Well, I expect they're heftily insured,' he adds.

Magda agrees.

But now Imelda appears carrying a small rucksack.

Tomasz gives her a smile. They've had the short argument about her insisting she doesn't want him to come with her, saying she'll back in a day or two.

But he has persuaded her to let him take her to the station in Edinburgh.

Imelda manages to get through the hugs and kisses from his sister and mother, which always make her uncomfortable, having had a non-kissed upbringing with her stern, cold father. She's managed to enjoy sex, but still has difficulty with the less physical side of relationships.

Magda and Helena wait on the balcony until they see his Land Rover come out on the bottom road and wave, knowing full well he won't be looking.

Magda's only just got back in the house, leaving her mother picking out early weeds, when the phone rings.

It's DI Walker.

After a clipped 'how are you', he asks her what she knows about the Turnbull family..

19

She pauses.

Does she want to do this?

She's well aware that anything to do with local clan relationships is always difficult, with rivalries and hatreds which have existed for hundreds of years . . . but the Turnbulls are particularly difficult being known for their treachery and backstabbing, according to her father anyway.

'Which ones?' she says knowing it makes a big difference with them.

'Big house up in the hills above Jedburgh,' he says, not knowing that it matters. 'Married to an American.'

She pauses.

She's met him once . . . which was enough. A loud voice and a boor were her mother's opinion and so they've never met him since, although apparently he's rarely at the big house – a bit of a world-wide operator. Most people appalled that such a nice lady like Catherine should have managed to think he was a suitable husband.

'Hello?' says Walker.

'Sorry,' says Magda, 'I've only met him the once . . .'

'And?' comes the abrupt response.

'Off the record? she asks.

'Of course,' he answers wearily.

'Well, he's American, loud and rather arrogant, but rich enough to be accepted by a lot of Border's folk.'

There's a pause.

'You mean the Border's 'royalty'?' he mutters.

She ignores the inappropriate word.

'If you mean the old local families . . . yes . . . why, what's happened?'

'There's been a break in – not sure yet how they got in, but safe opened and no prints.'

She waits, astonished, already thinking he's said too much.

'I could do with some help . . .' he adds quietly.

She takes the phone out to the balcony to give herself some her time.

'What sort of help?' she murmurs, her head filling with a dozen arguments.

Another pause.

'Well, there's no-one there, abroad apparently, finding it difficult to get any response.'

Magda hasn't any idea where they might be, she's heard very little.

'Doesn't Andrew Jardine have a contact?'

'You mean the caretaker? He's given us a couple of numbers but no response yet.'

'Well,' she says, 'I can't think of anyone else . . . since the remarriage they've become . . . well a bit . . . remote . . . literally. I think the husband works for an oil company.'

Walker waits.

'You could contact their solicitor,' she suggests.

'Any idea?'

'No . . . probably Hawick.'

Walker gives her a sigh and asks her to tell him if the Borders telegraph tells her anything.

She stands looking out at the other side of the valley.

Since her father died her connections to the 'telegraph' have become less communicative to her than him . . . being a woman and a police officer not the best qualifications to be kept in the loop.

But she does make a few calls, which confirm what she thought: 'an abominable man', 'what does she see in him?' and 'loud and rude' etcetera, which means of course that they've rarely accepted any invitations – which won't help DI Walker.

*   *   *

URSULA

Janet and I have been for a walk.
January is a cruel month.
Especially here in the Borders.

I can't remember a day when it didn't rain and Ziggy has confirmed that last autumn was one of the wettest on record and January hasn't fared much better until today.

A wall-to-wall blue sky, which meant quite a heavy frost at dawn . . . which was when she dragged me out of a warm bed for just a quick bowl of porridge before we're striding along beside the furious river.

Now you might think porridge wouldn't be my choice for breakfast, but you may have forgotten that my strait-laced Lancashire not-mother was of the same opinion as the Scots, but, of course, without any honey to sweeten the taste like Janet makes it.

Just after dawn is a good time to see the creatures who are struggling to keep alive in the cold and shorter days, including this morning the vivid flashes of kingfishers zigzagging from one bank to the other.

We get back to find that Ziggy has for once made the fire!! For which, Janet takes him a mug of coffee as he likes it. Black, 'ten' sugars.

She's just about to leave him to it but notices that he's looking at a huge mansion, a few outside views and then inside following a handheld camera upstairs and downstairs.

'Are you thinking of moving?' she asks.

He shakes his head – which makes his wig wobble – which makes her giggle.

'No way,' he mumbles, 'but it's an intriguing break-in.'

'When?'

By now I've tuned in and wander through to peep over her shoulder.

To arrive as the camera is going upstairs again.

A bit like Magda's house, but if anything even grander, which is difficult to believe. We watch as the camera goes into a number of huge rooms and then goes up another level.

The walls are covered with enormous paintings, mostly the usual highland cattle and scenic views mixed in with the family gatherings accompanied with the dead animals they've killed.

Ziggy then switches to a property site and quickly pulls up the house in question. Eight point five million for house and a large estate.

'This is only visible on US sites, nothing here in the UK,' he murmurs.

'Where is it? asks Janet.

A flurry of his fingers and a map appears and zooms into a town. Jedburgh. We've been. Not very big and Queen Mary's house was shut, but I quite liked it. Not as busy as Galashiels or as full of itself like Melrose.

But now he's showing us the house a good few miles up in the hills away from the town.

'The police are struggling to find out how they got in,' he tells us, 'only a hole in a window forty feet up from the ground.'

Janet sighs.

'Well, my money would be on an inside job . . . who owns it.'

Surprisingly it takes a few minutes before he can come up with a recent family photograph. A woman surrounded by ten or eleven children and other adults.

'I expect Magda will know them,' I venture.

But now Ziggy's lost interest in family photos and is searching a bewildering array of sites with lots of numbers and newspaper articles.

This is too much for me and Janet follows me back to the non-flickering living room.

She's standing at the window. I go to the kitchen to wash up.

I've never understood the desire to be rich and my not-mother was absolutely convinced it was the fastest way to hell and damnation.

*   *   *

Louisa insists on driving, because Fletcher knows she doesn't approve of his unhurried manner, which he has gradually adopted the further away he got from being a detective rushing from one place to another.

She crosses the Al which bypasses Berwick and goes down through the area south of the estuary which is lined with big sheds and yards. Then just when we can see the spires and buildings of the old town she takes a very sharp right and continues along past some docks and desolate land declared to be sold for new properties, but then along a main street which she tells us is called Spittal, which makes Fletcher smile, although it's evident desolation isn't inviting.

However the trick at the end of the village is a little zigzag which takes them to the beach.

With recognition built in eons ago Rollo is going berserk in the back, even before he can see it.

So it's a relief that the parking is only twenty yards to the promenade and then down to the sand.

Well, some sand, but mainly assorted collections of branches and other washed-up items, after all the storms we've been having.

This doesn't bother Rollo who insists on chasing sticks and digging holes and chewing seaweed as though he's been doing this all his life.

So it's best part of an hour before they go back and cross the high bridge into the town, where the next surprise awaits.

Even after the swiftly taken couple of dog legs Louisa takes, the other two begin to realise this isn't a car friendly place. Where there is parking it's ticket machines and there aren't any spaces anyway. But Louisa swishes down and comes out at a street back near the estuary, then swerves at the last turning left into a carpark and pulls up in space as though it was waiting for her.

She indicates the glove compartment to Fletcher who finds an old parking disc.

'It's two hours, so we'll be alright here, until we go up to the Barracks,' she says unbuckling her seat belt and getting out.

The other two follow her.

Ellie hanging on to the wet dog as he's ready for yet another excitement.

But then the three of them are disconcerted to see Louisa striding her way to the sign saying YHA.

Inside the guy at the counter greets her with a kiss on both cheeks a la francaise, while Ellie and Fletcher are introduced as a couple of ne'er-do-wells, who she's been landed with for no good reason.

And now they're sitting having excellent coffee and cakes.

'I thank you for not making any comment about my age in this establishment,' she murmurs, 'but as you can see most of the customers are of similar age or unlikely to ever need a bed here.'

Fletcher can only exchange a shake of the head with a grinning Ellie.

'Anyway,' Louisa continues, 'it's only a couple of corners and you're up on your walls, Eleanor.'

She's now getting out her book and opening a map.

Louisa points out where they are now and the steps which will take them up on to the wall and then changes her mind about meeting them back here and shows her where there's a gate which comes out at the Barracks.

Fletcher's staring at two beautiful Asian ladies who wouldn't have been extraordinary in the middle of Leicester, but here? In a YHA café?

Ellie's impatience means she and Fletcher are soon climbing some old steps onto the walls. She often sighs when visiting medieval buildings that they've lost their real jobs and are now just brief holiday entertainments, but obviously the walls are still keeping the sea at bay, even when it's a lazy day, no thundering waves crashing against them and in any case the waves will be mostly battering the long sea wall far out at the mouth of the estuary.

'So which bits did your man build then?' he asks.

She consults her map.

'Well, this bit for starters,' she mumbles, but is then transfixed by a dark figure up on one of the towers. For a moment she can't think what it is? A statue?

It isn't moving.

Rollo on the other hand is desperate to keep going, so she lets him pull her round the other side . . . where she realises it's just someone with a black anorak hood looking out to sea.

Fletcher on the other hand is staring down at the houses in the inner side. They're certainly not the same age as the wall. In fact it looks like they're very recent indeed.

She continues on towards the huge gun pointing out to sea, which checking her map, is apparently a Russian gun from the Crimean War.

But now also both of them realise that turning the corner means the paths are very icy, so they both gingerly step onto the grass, especially Ellie because Rollo keeps trying to look over the wall, which means she must give Fletcher the map.

The inside and outside continue to contradict each other.

On the inside there are allotments, whilst there's the remains of gun emplacements on the wall . . . a building looking like a church hall turns out to be an old 'magazine', whilst on the outside there are lots of grassed over ice houses.

But now they're reached one of the few entrances under the wall, which is called the 'Cowport', but no mention or sign of any cattle? Or Louisa's car.

And so they go through the gate to find there are two churches beside each other, the first St Andrews and then the Church of Scotland.

Ellie is keen to go into the first one, where there are a gaggle of closely packed eighteenth century gravestones, but there's a funeral in progress, whilst the other one's shut.

So, defeated by death, she's making her way to the library where she's found there is actually a town archive.

A lovely old lady on the counter, but she tells her the archivists are having their lunch, so that's another frustration.

And now they find Louisa reading the paper in the car as though this history all around her is of no significance at all.

Fletcher stands reading the notice by the gate on the barracks, which contradictorily says it's the HQ OF XY ETC.

But then Louisa decides she's had enough and tells them they'll have to go home.

*   *   *

As a bolt hole the little town at the end of the railway line is as out of the way as you can get in England.

So this threesome is happy to be infrequent returnees in the gaps in their itinerant lives.

This doesn't mean they don't get inquisitive looks and frowns, but Otka, the small one, with her blonde hair in a tight ponytail has chattered away in various shops about her 'sister' Voudra, who has very dark hair and their friend, Xavi, being acrobats, who frequently disappear to work in circuses and fairs all over the world . . . which is true.

But this is only true about their day jobs.

And what they do on their days off and often even while they're working would horrify them.

And this afternoon they are all lying on the same bed, their limbs intertwined and their sweat dribbling over each other's bodies. Once again they have forced or acquiesced in every sexual coupling two women and one man can imagine in a drug assisted orgy of pleasure and violent excess.

And it's also Otka who is the first to untangle herself from the knotted limbs to head for the shower after firing up the coffee machine.

And she's not surprised as she comes back to find Voudra in her favourite position riding Xavi like a rocking horse. She ignores them and puts the pan on the stove to heat the milk.

It's at this moment her mobile splutters and she eventually finds it on the floor and prods it.

The other two don't stop, so she goes into the front room and listens to the soft voice telling her what she was expecting.

'But that's only six hundred k for you, because a couple of the pieces, the Venetian glass bowls and the French necklace, are too famous for our usual customers . . . although I'm sure I can find someone soon.'

27

Otka says nothing and closes the phone.

'Hajzl!' she growls.

She glances over at the writhing bodies and, slugging the coffee back, stalks over to take out her anger on them.

*   *   *

At this time of year the birds who winter elsewhere haven't even had any yearning to come back to the pitches on the rock face.

But there are still the kingfishers, who, living up to their names, continue to hunt in the tumultuous rapids below and occasionally rest a while on one of the hawthorn branches or the tangled ivy hanging down.

Even more occasionally a mountaineering rodent finds its way into the cave only to come scurrying out again after a few dangerous minutes.

The short days mean that the cave only gets any direct sunlight for a few minutes late mid-morning which doesn't give much heat, so nothing much stirs in the dark wet cavities tunnelling back into the cliff upwards to the house above.

So, it's only the invertebrates who can survive in these temperatures and the dampness.

But . . . there is the creature, whose reasons and abilities to exist have somehow been conserved, who is now stirring.

There's a whispering and a muttering, some movements in the darkness.

Are those sounds words?

Water babbles, but this is harsher, rasping, shushing.

Silence - then a growl.

A cry of pain.

CHAPTER THREE

Imelda is standing on the beach.

Her favourite time.

Dawn.

And one of those soft mauve openings . . . which always somehow quietens the dawn chorus . . . although the gulls have no truck with that. Not when the competing currents are confusing the beach creatures and the other birds. Currents that come slicing towards each other having rounded the different sides of the island, although she knows the ones from the right are always going to overpower those from the left as they have the extra power of the open sea, whilst the left side is competing with the estuary.

Eventually she looks along towards the painter's house, which is the other side of the estuary.

She's arranged to meet the daughter at ten o'clock, so no rush.

But now she's thinking about the woman she's decided was her mother.

Another solitary, damaged person, which is why they were comfortable with each other, both preferring silence to conversation. Solitude to crowds. Both contemplating death as an escape from the chattering, intimacy and questions of the busy world. But she mentioned, only once, that she'd had a husband and a daughter, who sounded like the sort of people you wouldn't want to live with.

She looks again towards the far beach.

The woman's also probably the sort of person who believes in being on time for meetings and tuts when people are late.

This makes her smile.

Tomasz is not a solitary person, but he's no time for deadlines or meetings.

Which gives her a pang of . . . what? A realisation that he's the first person she's ever missed . . . when he's not here.

At first she's worried about that . . . but then she just smiles, and wonders whether she'll tell him?

An hour later she's across the estuary with wet feet and skirt, walking towards the ruined building and then realises there's a figure standing next to it looking in her direction. Now waving.
She doesn't deliberately slow her pace but that's what happens.

But the woman is still waving so she waves back, feeling awkward.

The meeting is cordial, even a bit wary.
Eventually as Imelda gets close enough the woman puts out her hand . . . so she grits her teeth and proffers her own.
Her's is cold and the other woman almost shivers.
'You must be a hardy soul,' she laughs, 'I guess you'd call me a soft sassenach.'
Imelda is hopeless at this sort of camaraderie even with people she's known for a long time. So she just shrugs.
This makes the other woman feel awkward, so Imelda manages a faint smile.
'Shall we go in? the woman asks, pulling her huge, obviously new coat to herself as though the gentle breeze is a gale.
They step carefully through the doorway and look at the dilapidated ruin.
Imelda is getting memories of the atmosphere of this house, the comfortable silences of their togetherness, just the soft scratchings of her brush or the sighs of disappointment as she cocked her head on one side while looking at the canvas.
This other woman worrying about her coat getting caught on the damaged cluttering of wind and rain swept furniture.
'I suppose it was . . . 'nice' when she was here,' murmured the woman.

Imelda looks out the window, wishing she hadn't come . . . even though she'd have missed the beach and the sea . . . and the light . . .

'By the way, my name is Christina and I'm married, so my surname is Thompson . . .'

Imelda looks away.

'So how did you meet?' the woman asks.

Imelda frowns, thinking where else would you meet someone here?

She shrugs.

The woman looks away.

'Look . . . all I want to know is what happened to her things . . . her painting stuff . . . her clothes?'

Imelda looks at her as though she's stupid and sweeps her hand across the debris.

'The sea . . . the wind . . . birds . . . people . . . who knows?' she murmurs.

Christina snorts in exasperation.

'But didn't someone, the neighbours, the police, the local council . . . someone . . . you . . . think to . . . do something?'

Imelda looks away.

The woman waits like she might do with a naughty child.

Imelda is thinking how to explain how private Hebrideans are but can't find the words . . . and in any case she wasn't here when she died.

The woman turns round in frustration and makes her way to the entrance as if she couldn't just walk through the gap in the wall.

'Where's the police station here?' she demands.

Imelda stares at her again, wondering whether there will still be anyone in Tarbert, but doubts it.

'I think you'll have to go to Stornoway,' she mutters.

'Where's that?'

'Lewis.'

The woman shakes her head.

'You mean there isn't one here?'

Imelda shrugs.

The woman stares at her in disbelief.

'You're lying!' she shouts.

Imelda gives her one more stare and walks away.

The woman stands watching her, then shouting at her to come back, but Imelda keeps going before wading through the estuary and reaching the other beach. Finds herself standing looking out at the island, shivering and shaking with anger . . . and then realises she needs Tomasz.

* * *

Walker is a bit fed up that he can't get any response from the family.

'Bloody rich people,' he grumbles after another futile phone call.

He looks down the list that the caretaker gave him and is refusing to try any of the numbers in the US, Brazil and China for god's sake.

'Who the hell does business with China?'

Gill can only shrug.

She's never been further south than Leeds and that was only when her mother had a Krag Mara exhibition match, which meant at least two big guys regretted even getting in the ring. One lasting literally about five seconds and the other tried dancing around more than an arm's length away, until she literally flew at him and knocked him into the crowd.

She shakes her head, thinking she needs to get some practice in.

But then Walker gets another call.

A soft voice, asking to speak to a Detective Walker.

Then he's listening very hard.

'So you can't come just now?' he asks.

There's more extended intent listening and then he sighs and ends the call.

Gill frowns at him.

'Bloody rich people', he mutters again. 'She's saying they're in Paris at the moment and can't come back before next week.'

Gill shrugs, thinking 'why should we bother then?'.

'But she's sending me a list of things which were in the safe.'

She shrugs again.

'Sounds like an insurance job to me, what do these people do? Have they even got jobs?'

Before he can answer that his phone burbles again.

He listens, walking this way and that like he does when he's fed up.

'What?'

Another frown.

'But how would they have got up to the window?'

He listens again and then laughs.

Closing the call he stands shaking his head.

'What?' Gill asks.

'We've to look for people who can fly!' he laughs.

Gill shrugs.

'You mean Batman?'

Walker laughs again.

'Apparently.'

They both frown, then Gill grins.

'Cirque de Soleil.'

''What . . . who?'

'They're on the TV.'

He frowns again, but now she's showing him their website.

'Four thousand people!' he gasps.

'Well, I imagine that's not just the actual acrobats, their equipment and crew would be over a hundred I reckon and I think they've got different groups all round the world,' she adds.

'Okay but why would they bother. Won't they be paid mega bucks?'

Gill shrugs.

'But there are lots of other smaller circuses I imagine.'

Walker shrugs back.

'Okay, pooter whiz, that's your job. I'm going to check the road cameras in the vicinity.'

Gill smiles, 'pootering' better than spending time with road cops.

*   *   *

Otka gets a call from one of their buyers, who she's sent photos of the 'items' for him to see.

He's the sort of old guy who never shows any emotion when it comes to buying, but the fact he's got back so quickly is a bit of a giveaway.

No greetings just straight to business.

'I don't want to know how or where you got these items, but I can relieve you of them fairly quickly . . .'

She waits.

'So, come on, you know you can't go to the open market with these . . . and you'd probably be better off making an arrangement with the owners, who I assume won't be asking the police for help . . .'

She sighs.

'But you still want them?'

She can hear his laboured breathing which is a strong clue about their worth.

'The best thing you could do is leave them somewhere and contact the family . . . my bet is that they're not insured . . . the last recorded sighting of them is hundreds of years ago.'

She waits.

'The Venetian bowls belonged to Elizabeth the First and the necklace was given to her elder sister Mary by the King of France.'

'Okay, you ask around and come back with a figure,' she whispers and ends the call.

As it happens she's on the beach, so she keeps going . . . and finds herself running like a maniac, not even stopping as she splashes through the stream where it meets the waves.

She continues on until she gets to the rocks at the southern end of the beach under the cliffs and gasping for breath, stands with hands on knees.

As soon as she'd realised what they were she knew this would be very dangerous . . . having met the husband and seen his temper, she knew they were in real danger. The thought of even trying to deal with him was not possible.

She'd seen how he treated his wife . . . and her daughters . . . and another woman who was staying at the house for Christmas. He's a violent, misogynistic monster.

She realises she's staring into a rock pool and notices a crab scuttling along a few inches at a time . . . but then she jumps as a pair of claws comes scything out, grabs the little crab and as quickly disappears.

She's not one for omens, but . . .

Back at the house she finds Voudra sprawled across the settee reading a book, while she can hear Xavi's music playing upstairs meaning he's in the bath.

She flops down opposite her and sighs.

Voudra looks over her glasses.

'Result?' she asks.

'Not really.'

Now Voudra sits up.

'Why? What's the problem?'

'The Venetian bowls and the necklace won't be insured because they're priceless . . .'

'And?'

She glares at her.

'Henry Grey says it's likely that they belonged to royalty, so they won't be telling the police about those items and so that evil bastard will be hiring some very nasty people to find us.'

'Which royalty?'

'Elizabeth the First and her sister Mary.'

'Really? When was that?'

'Sixteenth century,'

'Ah . . .' says Voudra, sighs and sets off to the drinks trolley.

An hour later the three of them are sitting at the table.

Xavi is sitting half naked just a towel wrapped around his waist.

Voudra has stopped asking questions or suggesting solutions, which is always her way.

'What if we put them back?' mumbles Xavi.

Otka shakes her head.

'No, I think he'd still come after us.'

The silence allows them to hear the grandfather clock ticking ominously, the one they couldn't resist rescuing a couple of years ago, which still makes them smile when they think of how they did it.

'I know,' whispers Voudra, 'why don't we tell Henry to put them somewhere and then anonymously tell the police where they are?'

Otka grimaces, but Xavi shrugs.

But then she reminds them what the husband's like.

'It's not the money or their worth, it's that someone has taken something from him that will make him come looking for us.'

*　　　*　　　*

URSULA

Ziggy is getting excited.

I know this because of the shouting and blasphemies are getting louder and things being thrown about.

Out of curiosity I take him a coffee, which of course, he ignores, but I couldn't help seeing that he seems to be looking at jewellery . . . old stuff, things which really rich people used to wear . . . although of course they still do on 'occasions'.

And I also realise that he's in touch with that young woman, Ellie, so it must be something medieval.

I stand listening at the door.

'You're kidding!' he shouts.

I can't resist and quietly go back in behind him.

I never know which screen I need to look at, because there's three, no four, flickering away and one of them is Ellie's face. She's looking down at something but then looks up, her eyes bright with excitement.

'Yeh, I think I'm right,' she says.

I take a step forward and see that on another screen there's a picture of a necklace. Lots of huge red stones set on a gold chain. Looks heavy for putting round your neck, but the stones are amazing.

'So have these been handed down in the family?' asks Ziggy.

'Ah . . . that's where it gets tricky,' she murmurs.

Ziggy is bringing up bewildering sets of pictures and sections of books.

'Have you heard of the 'Rough Wooing'?

Even I find that a bit funny, imagining women being kidnapped and screaming for help, but probably giggling inside.

Ziggy pulls up the title and I can see it was when the Tudors were on the throne, not a period I know well at all.

'Short version?' says Ellie and assumes we're interested, so she rattles on.

'I'll start with the Romans because even you know they built Hadrian's wall to keep the Scots out – a bit more complicated than that, but then there was the Angles, Vikings and then the Normans. So Berwick was always being attacked from one side or the other . . . this went on until James the First, 1603, BUT not before the Tudors spent all their money on Berwick's walls, even though they were never finished . . . and the man who made a large amount of that money was Sir Richard Lee, who designed and built the walls that still exist today . . .' she sighs '. . . which is why I'm so interested in him.'

*   *   *

Ellie can't put up with Ziggy's butterfly approach to everything, fluttering from one shiny bit to another, so she puts him on silent . .

. and bottom of the screen because he'll be sharing images as well.

After an hour of diligent but frustrating investigation, she swears in exasperation and goes to see what the two oldies are up to.

Louisa seems to be writing a letter, as in on actual paper and an old-fashioned pen document, glasses perched on the end of her nose. Suppressing a giggle, Ellie sidles up to glance at the paper, headed of course, and marvels at the handwriting, which she thinks might be called Gothic by her computer.

Louisa sighs.

'Yes, I'm writing a letter, with a fountain pen, as I was taught at boarding school many years ago.'

Ellie supresses a smirk, trying to picture Louisa as a girl . . . tall, long golden tresses and court shoes.

But she sidles away to where Fletcher is dozing in an armchair.

He grins, but his eyes are shut.

'Ask who the poor beggar is who will be at the receiving end of this letter,' he mumbles.

Ellie sits on the plumfy sofa and dares to put her legs up . . . after removing her shoes. Rollo who'd come galloping in with her, glances at her and then at Louisa, who doesn't say anything, so he leaps onto the sofa with Ellie. He still isn't entirely sure it's permissible because most of the other furniture is definitely out of bounds.

'If you must know it's about the state of the grounds of Norham Castle after a busload of school kids from Newcastle or somewhere had been let loose and apart from the binloads of litter, some of them thought it would be good idea to climb on the walls and cause a landslide.'

'So why are you writing the letter? Were you there?' asks Ellie.

'No . . . but I'm chair of the 'Friends of the Castle' and Alice has asked me to pen one.'

'Wonderland comes to the Borders,' muttered Fletcher, which earned him the look over her glasses, which always makes Ellie giggle.

'I didn't know you did that?' asks Ellie, 'you've never suggested we go there.'

'Hum . . . well . . . actually I can't stand the woman, no idea how she got the job, a card-carrying philistine, only marginally better than the kids.'

But now Ellie's on her phone.

'Aha, as I thought, part of the Border fortifications built by the Tudors, so maybe my man was part of that, I'll have to check it out.'

'Well,' says Louisa, 'would you like to do the tour with the 'Chair of the Friends'?' she asks with a supercilious smile.

'How gracious,' replies Ellie with another giggle.

'Fletcher, the carriage, at the double.'

He attempts to leap to his feet but falls over and ends up on all fours.

Louisa sighs.

'In your own time,'

An hour later they're standing on some battlements looking across the river.

They had to meet Alice, who wasn't so bad, but she was obviously terrified of Louisa and embarrassingly subservient.

Fletcher is frowning and then points at the large house on the other side of the river high above some rocks and the thrashing water.

'Is that . . ?'

Louisa shakes her head.

'I'm afraid it is . . . Lubavaine, where that terrible man met his justified desserts.'

Ellie frowns at both of them.

'Um,' says Louisa. 'Not exactly a bedtime story, but I'll give you the edited version when we get back.'

*　　　*　　　*

Voices

I can hear voices?

Children?

No, that was another time . . . screaming, shouting and then a single voice . . . a woman cursing, although I couldn't make out the words. Might be English?

Quiet now.

I miss my daughter.

Mary.

Long dark hair.

I hope she's safe.

I'm cold . . . so cold . . . and wet.

But there is light, a glimmering over there.

Maybe . . . if it wasn't for these shackles . . .

I can't believe it, the one round my left wrist has just fallen off, rusted away . . . now the other! And now my ankles . . . I'm free!!!

Careful, quietly . . . although, I haven't seen a guard since . . . when . . .

I crawl towards the light . . .

I can feel the wind . . .

The light is so bright . . .

So bright . . .

CHAPTER FOUR

Walker gets a call.

He doesn't catch the name, but quickly realises who it is.
The American.

So he listens while the guy berates him, the rest of the
police force, the Scots, the 'bastards' who've broken into his home
and why hasn't he caught anyone yet?

It's not as if he's never been sworn at by members of the
public and some very nasty villains before and he did grow up on
a Manchester estate . . . in fact he's just surprised that his colour
hasn't been mentioned so far.

So he holds the phone away from his ear until the noise
abates.

'Sorry, sir, who are you?'

'Who the hell do you think I am?'

'Well . . . until you tell me, I don't know.'

There's another bout of expletives, which finishes with the
predictable threat to contact his superiors, so Walker is happy to
give him their telephone numbers, but then ends the call.

Gill smirks at him.

'That sounds like an angry man!'

Walker laughs.

'You're not wrong, far above our paygrade, so I passed him
on.'

Gill shrugs.

'Can't see Edinburgh sending any reinforcements,
whatever grade.'

Walker shakes his head.

'As if I care.'

The two of them are in a car park in Jedburgh having a
coffee from the café, while the locals criss-cross the rugby pitch to
a path by the river.

Not a town either of them know, although when she checks she tells him the police station isn't manned at weekends.

'What?' he frowns. 'Isn't that when most crimes are committed?'

'Nah,' she continues,' apparently it's just the local Sheriff's Court, so it's only busy Wednesday and Thursday.'

They watch as one after another people come to walk their dogs.

'I wouldn't fancy playing rugby on that pitch, it'll be covered with dogshit.'

Gill looks at him.

'Didn't have you down as a rugby player or even a supporter.'

Walker shakes his head and smirks.

'Cricket's my game, don't think they play it up here.'

She frowns.

'I think there's a pitch at Melrose.'

Walker shrugs, looks at his phone and ignores the call.

Gill looks away.

'If he's calling me from Singapore, I think we can assume he's not about to appear . . . and the coverage here is so poor anyway.'

But then there's another call.

He listens.

No shouting.

'So where are you?'

'Okay, we're on our way.'

Gill waits.

'That was the wife, soft spoken and polite . . . how on earth did she get married to that loudmouth?'

Gill shakes her head.

'Money?'

It's only twenty minutes away and he parks up next to an ancient Citroen.

They hadn't really taken in the view before although today they can see why someone would want to build a house here. The view is breath taking.

They climb the ten steps to the front door, which is opened as they get there.

A young woman, not the wife, smiles and invites them in.

'Mother is in the sitting room,' she gestures and sets off across the huge entrance hall.

They'd looked in there before so they know what it's like, three or four settees and a few armchairs as well. Huge paintings on the walls, small tables everywhere, all cluttered with vases and statuettes and other knick-knacks.

A tall slim woman stands up as they enter.

'Catherine Turnbull,' she says quietly.

Walker introduces himself and Gill.

She indicates a couple of armchairs, which they both find uncomfortably low.

'Tea, or coffee,' she asks as she returns to the chair she was sitting on.

Walker asks for coffee, black, whilst Gill shakes her head.

The daughter disappears.

There's an awkward few moments.

'I think my husband may have contacted you?' she smiles.

Walker shrugs and nods.

The woman smiles again.

'Patience not one of his virtues I'm afraid.'

Walker grins.

'I come from a very rough part of Manchester . . . and I'm black, so . . .'

The woman frowns.

There is another uneasy pause.

'Are you aware of what's been taken?' he asks, thinking he can't be bothered with all these pauses.

'Um, yes, Anne has made a list with photographs.'

Now he sees there's a file lying on the low table in front of him.

He picks it up and riffles though the six or seven pages of photographs of plates, jugs and vases . . . and then pieces of jewellery, noticing the valuations in small numbers beneath each piece . . . and then there's a list, including a grand total.

He looks up at her, trying not to give any inclination of what he thinks about so much wealth.

'And they are all insured?'

Catherine stares at him.

'Yes . . . but frankly many of them are priceless, some of them hundreds of years old.'

Walker passes the list to Gill, who tries not to be astounded and fails, but is saved by the return of the daughter.

She places the tray with a plate of biscuits on the table in front of Walker and goes to stand looking out the bay window.

Walker reaches for the cup, realising they're not getting the best crockery.

Gill has the odd sense of being invisible, which she's not that unhappy about, as it means she can watch the scene unfold like in an old-fashioned play.

The pause is awkward . . . like whoever's got the next line has forgotten it or is gauging the audience's liking for suspense.

'My stepfather thinks he should employ his own investigators,' the daughter murmurs without turning round.

Her mother shakes her head and smiles at Walker.

'My husband comes from Los Angeles . . . and he . . . likes 'to solve his own problems'.'

Walker tries to give her a stern look but realises she's not smiling anymore.

'I've tried to explain about the British attitude . . . but . . .'

He manages a smile.

'Well . . . my superior is a bit like that as well . . . so hopefully we can get a result . . . soon.'

She smiles again but it soon fades.

44

Walker smiles back, takes a sip of the coffee and places it back on the tray.

'So you decided not to extend the alarm system to the second floor,' he asks.

She looks away.

'He didn't think it necessary . . . second floor up and all the alarms in the grounds seemed enough . . . and how could they be certain that it wasn't alarmed?'

Walker nods.

'So who knew about the alarm system? Where the safe was? What was in it?'

She stares at him, the first sign of anxiety?

'Well . . .' she begins, then falters. 'I suppose he and I . . . Maggie . . .'

Walker waits.

'She's . . . my . . . housekeeper.'

He nods, wondering what that might entail.

'But didn't you have a house full over the Christmas period?'

She nods.

'Most of them were in the annexe,' interrupts Anne, 'ensuite rooms, so no need to go upstairs here.'

'Annexe?' he asks wondering why he hadn't realised there was one.

'It's behind the house, accommodates up to twenty people, although some of my friends were sleeping in the bunkhouse as well.'

'So quite a crowd?' he smiles.

'Yes, with all the staff there were over sixty of us.'

'Staff?'

'Well, most of them were just for the Christmas week and they came in from the town or the hostel.'

'So who had access to the second floor?'

Catherine shrugs.

'Well, none of them really, there are washrooms on the ground floor and the first floor they could use, but . . .'

He waits.

'It wasn't locked, if that's what you're thinking . . .'

He smiles.

She frowns again.

'The safe was hidden and it was locked . . .'

Walker lets the pause lengthen.

'So who knew the code?'

She shakes her head.

'Just me and my husband.'

Walker couldn't help glancing at the daughter, who smiles back at him and shakes her head.

He looks back at the mother, who looks away.

He waits again.

He can see she's determined not to cry, to show any weakness.

'As I said, some of the items have been in my family for hundreds of years . . . they're priceless, historic artefacts . . . no-one could display them without someone recognising them . . . so . . .'

Walker nods but knows he's no idea about things being in the same family for more than one generation, never mind his family have anything needing insurance.

'But there are people who would 'covet' them.'

He turns to look at the daughter, who's glaring at him.

'My 'stepfather' knows some people and he's employing them to hunt them down.'

Walker frowns at her, the sarcasm disfiguring her face.

'He doesn't think you can find them, he's the sort of person who thinks he's above the law.'

But then she sighs and 'flounces' out of the room.

Walker looks at Gill, who shrugs to hide the need to giggle at such over the top amdram behaviour.

Catherine shakes her head.

'I'm afraid they've never got on.'

Walker wants to ask how she 'gets on' with him but thinks not just now.

'Is there anything else you can tell us?'

Catherine stares at him.

He realises her eyes are very pale blue.

She shakes her head.

'So just to be clear, the hired in staff didn't go upstairs?'

She nods.

'What about your other visitors?'

She shakes her head again.

'They'd no reason either, as I said, there are two bathrooms on the first floor and they could go back to the annexe if they needed anything.'

'How many staff?'

She shakes her head.

'Ten or twelve.'

'Local?'

'Most of them but some were hired through a firm in Melrose.'

She reaches over to one of the side tables and finds a card which she offers to him.

He takes it and hands it to Gill.

'I've also put the details of the safe installers, I'm afraid they only have offices in Edinburgh and Glasgow.'

Walker has had enough.

'Can we take another look at the room with the safe again,' he asks.

She smiles and stands up.

'Of course.'

*　　　*　　　*

Magda puts her phone down.

'My, my,' she whispers to herself, but then realises that both her mother and her brother are staring at her.

'What?' she asks.

Helena continues to stare at her, but Tomasz is grinning.

'They can't manage without you?' he laughs.

She looks away.

'It's the burglary at Catherine Turnbull's, DI Walker's having trouble with the aristocratic reluctance to talk . . . although it's more probably the American husband wanting to hire his Mafia friends to do the job.'

Tomasz frowns, he's never met the man, just heard people using the same epithets – 'a loudmouth and a bully'.

'Really?'

'Well, he's somewhere else at the moment, Singapore, I think.'

'Best place for him,' growls Tomasz, recalling a rather dismal weekend trailing a woman he'd met in Istanbul.

'You're not going are you?' asks Helena with a reluctant sigh.

Magda makes a face.

'I'm worried about Catherine . . . Anne as well.'

Tomasz frowns again.

'Why?'

Magda goes to look out the window.

'You shouldn't have to lie about the bruises on your arms and your neck . . . if you are happily married . . . should you?'

'Really,' he asks, but then Helena has gone to put her arm round Magda.

'I saw them too,' she says giving Tomasz a glare.

Tomasz frowns.

'It's not your job anymore,' he grumbles, 'why don't you tell DI Walker?'

Magda sighs.

'Okay, I will . . . but I've said I'll meet her for a coffee in half an hour in Jedburgh.'

'Right,' says Tomasz, 'I've got to go to Edinburgh to fetch Imelda, but when we're back . . .'

He realises that both Magda and his mother are giving him the same stare, so he shakes his head and laughs.

'Message received . . . I'll put myself in the reserve team.'

Both Magda and Helena can't help laughing at that, so he sets off, in time to give way to Amelia and two of her tribe coming back from the school run.

Amelia looks after him and then at Magda and her mother, clocks the serious faces and sighs.

'I thought you'd retired?' she demands.

'Um,' mutters Magda, 'this is the women's war, I can't retire from that.'

Catherine was late, wearing a cardigan despite the heat.

Magda has called DI Walker who was initially hesitant until she told him about the bruises,

'I can't say I'm surprised and the daughter was twitchy as well,' he muttered, 'so see what you can find out. I'm not keen on people shouting at me on the phone.'

Catherine didn't want to meet in their usual busy café, so they were in one of the side rooms in the Station Hotel, which was as empty as usual.

They'd hardly kissed but before they sat down, Catherine pulls up her sleeve to show her a huge purple bruise on her forearm.

'On my back as well,' she whispers, tears starting to run down her cheeks.

Magda wants to hug her, but has second thoughts, given the bruises.

'You need to go to your doctor and then your solicitor . . . no, better than that, I'll take you to Gala to see Jennifer Holroyd..'

Catherine is shaking her head and crying.

Magda realises this is the breaking of a dam, probably a long time coming.

She puts her arms round her and lets her put her head on her shoulder.

A waitress appears, clocks the picture, and backs out.

This lasts for a good five minutes, until Catherine blows her nose three or four times and manages a feeble smile.

'Ironic,' she mutters, 'the number of times you cried on my shoulder.'

Magda grins.

'Well, I never thought I would be reciprocating, you were always so strong.'

The waitress peers round the corner.

Magda beckons her in.

'We'll have two Americano's and two tots of Clynelish, please,' she whispers.

The waitress nods and disappears.

And then the story unfolds.

Mostly sexual to start with, but recently more unpredictable.

'I don't know whether it's to do with his financial dealings, he's never talked about them other to claim he's one of the richest men in the world – which is obviously not true, just his ego.'

Magda nods, she's overheard him bragging at events and gatherings, which she just assumed was what Americans are like.

'But . . . the worst thing is that I think he's started on the girls.'

Magda stares at her.

'Are you sure . . . that's not acceptable . . . in fact it's criminal,' she says, looking round to see no-one's hearing this.

'I think he started with Mary, but she's back at Uni now.'

'How do you know?'

'I heard her shouting at him and when I went to find them, he just said he was teasing her and seemed sorry.'

'What did Mary say?'

She smiled sadly.

'She just said next time she'd have her hockey stick.'

Magda waits.

Catherine stares at a painting on the wall..

'And now with the robbery he's really angry, vowing to kill whoever did it. Doesn't want to talk to the police. Says he 'knows people, who will take care of it and that the people who broke in will wish they'd never done it, before they die'.'

Magda is astounded. She doesn't like him, but this . . .

She doesn't really know what to say and starts worrying about what Tomasz will say or do, when he hears about it.

'Has he said when he's coming back?'

'No, but he'd said he'd be away for three or four months . . . I can't remember where he was going after Singapore . . . the US I expect.'

Magda reaches out and holds her hands.

'Look, the first thing, you and Anne must come to live with us, Tomasz is fetching Imelda from Edinburgh, he'll be back by four.'

Catherine's shaking her head, but Magda gets up and taking her arm, sets off to her car.

Back at the house after collecting Anne and two suitcases of clothes each, they arrive back to find Tomasz and Helena having G&Ts on the terrace.

Explanations are given and Helena takes Anne off to make a meal.

Magda can't help glancing at Tomasz, who gives her a weary smile.

'Can't shoot him from here, I'm afraid,' he shrugs.

Magda shakes her head.

'Uhuh, but what can we do?'

Catherine sighs.

'I'm sorry to foist my troubles on you,' she whispers.

'You didn't,' says Magda . . . 'but you do need to talk to your lawyers. After all the house and most of what's been stolen belongs to you . . . your family, for hundreds of years.'

Catherine nods, but now Tomasz shrugs again.

'I wouldn't count on any of that, I imagine he has a string of very powerful lawyers.'

This results in a long, uncomfortable silence.

Surprisingly it's broken by the least likely voice . . . Imelda's.

'He's dead now, but I used to know an old guy who had the sort of contacts who would know if these things were being offered for purchase.'

Magda and even Tomasz are astonished, one of the longest sentences either of them have ever heard her say, but then he remembers she knew Roper, the old guy living in squalor in the basement of a house on Carlton Hill in Edinburgh . . . 'knew' as in 'carnally' . . . well, in sexual activity which would be beyond Magda's imagination.

He sighs.

'Yeh, but I think he took all those connections with him.'

Imelda gives him a blank look.

'So how did an old man, who didn't have a phone, who couldn't walk, couldn't even stand up, do business with people who would never have gone to his flat?' she whispers.

Magda glances at Tomasz . . . she knew that's where they first met up.

'He didn't,' whispers Tomasz looking at her, 'because you were his runner.'

She nods.

'Not the only one, but yes . . .'

'So . . ?' Magda asks, wondering now that's she's retired that she can actually listen to this.

Tomasz is still frowning at Imelda.

'And one of them doesn't even live in Edinburgh, he's in Berwick. I've been there. A huge house on the walls, looking out at the sea.'

Magda is aghast, she's never heard Imelda say so many words, but what she's saying is even more astonishing.

'What's he called?' she asks, thinking of her father, who would often visit friends there, people who rarely came here and then realising she can't remember any names either.

Imelda looks away.

Magda glances at her mother, who is stony faced.

'He never took me there,' she asserts, 'he said they were 'ne'er do wells' and 'not proper company for a lady',' which makes her laugh.

'Well,' says Tomasz, interrupting the following silence, 'that sounds like a plan.'

Everyone else frowns at him, but gradually they all realise that it's the only one on the table.

*   *   *

URSULA

'Very little to be honest,' murmurs Ziggy, looking a bit worried, which is actually quite scary on a clown face. I've always been frightened of them . . . my mother again, telling me: 'they're the work of the devil', which was one of the few things she said that I believed to be true.

He's talking to Tomasz, who's given him a name, someone in Berwick.

'Give me a couple of hours, I'll have to go deep,' he mutters and for a moment his fingers are still . . . in itself a very rare event.

He leans back in the chair.

'Where's Janet?' he asks.

'I'm here,' she says, having crept up behind me.

'Fancy a protection job?' he asks, as he turns round.

She stares at him.

'Who and from who?' she asks.

I think it should be 'whom', but the seriousness of their two faces makes that pretentious.

'Tomasz and Imelda.'

She frowns.

'I can't imagine anyone trying to take them on . . . one of them could kill you when you wouldn't know he was even there and the other is really weird.'

'No, not them, a friend of theirs, the woman whose house was burgled.'

She looks at me. I've no idea either.

So he tells us.

And now we're on the way to the seaside.

*   *   *

The show had gone well, although Voudra is rubbing her shoulder.

Xavi cautiously approaches her.

'I'm sorry,' he whispers.

Voudra grins.

'Not your fault, I was too quick,' she sighs.

He's still looking fearful; he's been too often on the end of her savage tongue.

But now she's hugging him and whispering in his ear.

He laughs.

Otka is on her laptop, her face very serious.

'We're in trouble, guys,' she whispers.

The other two stop laughing and turn to look at her.

'What?' asks Voudra.

'It's Ronald . . . he's telling me that the word is out. The American husband wants to know who did the job. He's offering a million dollars for our names and where we are.'

Voudra goes to look at the screen.

'Has Ronald shown anything to anyone else.'

'Only one guy, who lives in Berwick . . . but he thinks he's not offered them up yet and he's scared.'

'So what do we do next?'

'Well, Ronald says to stay low, disappear for now.'

Voudra sighs.

'We can't really get out of the Prague Festival; they'd never forgive us.'

The other two exchange glances.

Otka looks back at her laptop.

'I'll tell Ronald to hide the stuff, go to his house on the Vienne or somewhere else.'

Three naked bodies glistening with sweat which has now gone cold.

They shiver.

*   *   *

The wind.

I can feel the wind.

I look down at my hands.

I stare at them.

They look very old . . . but they're not just bones.

The flesh is white . . . no, there are pink bits on the knuckles.

My arms are thin, but again they have flesh.

Now as the sun comes across from above the trees over the other side of the river, I can feel and see that my body is shivering.

I'm alive!

Without thinking, I look round for some clothes.

There's a brown lump of material by the wall.

I scramble over to it, my knees and legs all trembly, but now I can see it's a sort of coat . . . no it's a robe . . . like a monk would wear . . . I struggle to get into it, shivering with the cold and the excitement.

Eventually I'm all wrapped up and huddled in a corner until the shivering gets less.

But all the time thinking I must be dreaming.

I thought I was dead.

And now I can hear voices.
*I shuffle towards the entrance . . . feeling the
wind more and more . . . until I get to the edge of
the cave.*

*The sunlight is in my eyes, it's so bright I can
hardly see.*
But now as I shade my eyes I can see people.
Three or four.
*They're moving slowly, carefully, along the
rocks. They're over the other side of the river, which
is rushing and tumbling between us.*
The noise is deafening.
*I think I might shout, but then they wouldn't
hear me and . . . they could be Scots or other
soldiers - difficult to see.*
*I hide at the edge of the cave and watch them
crawl and climb along until they disappear behind
a bend in the cliffs.*

I realise I've been holding my breath.
My breath!??

I'm alive!!!

CHAPTER FIVE

Ellie has been doing some more research, while Louisa has taken a grumpy Fletcher to Edinburgh for an evening meal and a stopover in some posh hotel. No reason given?

So she's lost in the complications of the 'Rough Wooing'. Normally a timeline would help, but she's scrunched up two versions already. Rollo has left his usual place by her feet to hunker down on a sofa . . . one ear cocked in case the 'wicked witch' returns.

So as far as she can confirm that this Richard Lee was a bit of a villain, into cutting corners, but making sure he got most of the funds. In fact by the time he'd finished he had spent most of Elizabeth's money . . . and all to no avail because she was succeeded by James the First which made the protection largely unnecessary. This was also helped by the French getting bogged down in the religious wars of the next century.

Lee died in 1567 and somehow or another managed to have spent all this money, so his two daughters had to get wed to survive.

His coffin was a grand affair, with a full-length body on top, with what was unlikely to have been lifelike, but now disappeared and local historians in St Albans not that interested. All his old houses in ruins for a long time.

So back tracking to when he was pocketing Elizabeth's money instead of on the walls, she gets wrapped up in the court rolls and financial records, which makes her head hurt. She knows she's hopeless with money herself, so in the end she goes for a drive.

Finds herself in Norham on the other side of the river from Lubavaine, the house where she was incarcerated and left to die. She's goes to stand on the bank opposite it, where she can see the cliffs beneath it and shudders at what happened. Where that terrible man who had locked them in had fallen to his death.

The rapids are not too ferocious, but she knew it would be really dangerous to try to get over to the other side, so just stands there, while Rollo keeps pushing the stick he's found wanting her to throw it.

But when she looks downstream she's spies a thin figure. Someone stumbling about on the rocks dangerously near to the rushing water. Too far away for her to make out what he or she's doing but knowing it's very foolhardy.

She wishes she'd brought her binoculars, but then there's a man standing a bit further upstream using his to look the opposite direction.

She goes to him and asks if she can borrow them, but by the time she can focus on where she saw him, he's disappeared.

'Did you see him?' she asks the man.

'Who?'

'Over there, on the rocks by the rapids.'

The man takes his binoculars back and trains them where she told him.

'Nah,' he mutters, 'and anyway, it's not really possible to get along on that section except when the river's really low . . . late summerish.'

She frowns.

He laughs.

'Yer seeing ghosts?'

She looks away.

She doesn't want to engage with that . . . she knows she's seen ghosts before, but no-one, even Fletcher, believes her.

But she's sure there was someone there.

And weirdly she thinks that he was wearing a monk's habit.

And then she remembers she's supposed to be going to the Berwick library to look at what the archivist has found for her.

After twenty minutes of furious driving she's rushing along the road to the library, which is housed in a fairly new council building, where, surprisingly, dogs are allowed.

The section where people can look at books and records that can't be taken out is half full. People, mostly old folk, smile at her and the woman at the desk has the pile of records and pamphlets they've found for her.

But after of an hour or so, she's not found out much more than she already knows, which is disappointing . . . although it all confirms Lee's venality.

She knows from her previous work, that medieval records are riddled with cover-ups and misinformation composed by clerks and officials all on the make . . . and the Tudors were the worst . . . although considering the current UK government, not much has changed . . . even a died-in-the-blue cynic like Louisa knows that.

So she finds herself back on the wall again, standing by the guns, the one from the Crimean War – definitely not her period. It's a calm day and the sea is way beyond the breakwater out in the estuary, which makes the walls seem very landlocked, which makes her wonder what it was like in Lee's time.

But then there's a voice calling her.

It's Tomasz . . . and surprisingly Imelda, who's looking less out of place than usual . . . even smiling! Is that a first?

And then there's hugs, like they've not met up for ages. Even Imelda! And what a hard muscled body she has!

And, of course, this makes Rollo very excited and does his 'turning on a sixpence' routine.

'So . . . what brings you here?' she asks.

'Ah . . .' murmurs Tomasz and leans on the wall, while Imelda turns away to stare at a row of three elegant Georgian houses – all of which seem to be empty. No curtains.

'We're meeting up with Becket and what's her name . . . Ursula . . .'

And there they are coming towards them.

So lots more hugs, but then Tomasz explains what's going on.

About the robbery and the husband being a vile American and Magda rescuing the wife.

Whilst Ellie is intrigued with this she can't avoid noticing the odd behaviour between Imelda and Ursula . . . which shouldn't have been that surprising given they're both weird people, with unbelievable backstories. It's as though it's the opposite of 'opposites don't attract'. Although they're both standing to one side and looking away, there's a strange tension emanating from them, which means she only hears some of what's Tomasz is saying.

'Anyway,' he interrupts her thinking, 'I don't think we can go in mobhanded like this . . .'

Imelda nods and speaks!

'Definitely not,' she murmurs. 'Just me.'

This is so finite that the rest of them set off to the YHA café and told not to expect a quick response.

So, Ellie gets to hear more details about the robbery and the husband's response.

'But now it's getting more worrying,' continues Tomasz, because the guy that Imelda's gone to see has . . . shall we say . . . possible access to the 'valuables'.'

Ellie frowns.

'What do you mean?'

Tomasz smiles. A cold smile.

'He's been asked to sell them on by the burglars.'

'Oh,' she whispers, not sure how that works.

'The problem is that there are least two pieces which are priceless. A necklace of rubies given to the Countess by Mary Queen of Scots and two glass bowls from Elizabeth the First,' he whispers back.

Her eyes go wide.

'Wow!' she gasps.

Tomasz puts his fingers to his lips and sits back in the chair.

'Scary, eh,' he adds.

But then Ellie frowns again.

'But how does Imelda . . ?'

He shakes his head.

'Long story . . . she knew a guy called Roper, who was . . . in the 'bring and buy' trade for stolen trinkets and paintings etcetera . . . now deceased . . . rather horribly, actually.'

'Ah . . . the man in Carlton Terrace?'

'The same.'

'You two!' says Becket.

They both stare at her.

She laughs.

'Thick as thieves doesn't cover it,' she adds with a malicious grin.

'So why . . .' murmurs Ellie.

'Same business, but expert in all things Elizabethan Berwick, apparently.'

She leans back in her chair, thinking 'how can she get to meet him'.

'Your period further back than her, I think?' says Tomasz.

She smiles.

'Well . . . as it happens I've recently become interested in the history of Berwick . . . especially in the sixteenth century . . . I've just come back from perusing the archives of that period.'

He stares at her.

She bursts out laughing, but then realises other café patrons are looking at them.

Becket and Ursula have been listening to this exchange but now all four of them realise they're causing a bit of an atmosphere and decide without speaking to get up and go.

Tomasz stands in the carpark not sure what to do.

So he lets Ellie take him up through the town, whilst Becket says she and Ursula will meet them at the Barracks . . . which tells Ellie she's been here before.

'Someone must have suffered,' she whispers to Tomasz as they set off up the hill.

*   *   *

Voudra is looking out of the plane window. Xavi is playing on his phone with earphones in.

She nudges him & nods at the window.

'Nearly there,' she mutters and pokes the curled up Otka who's crunched in the foot well between them, covered with a blanket, so nosy hostesses couldn't see her. For a person who has no fear of heights – or for that matter falling off trapezes and other structures and never broke a single bone – she hates flying or to be more precise flying in a plane.

She comes up like a seal and sighs.

'How long?'

'Five minutes to landing, half an hour to the taxi – maybe an hour to the hotel.'

Otka shivers.

It's actually only an hour and Otka is visually relieved that's all 'over and done with' which annoyingly she always sings out loud, even though she and Xavi are sitting at a table outside the hotel waiting for their drinks to arrive.

Upstairs Voudra has been trying to get updates from their potential buyers but coming up totally blank . . . which is very worrying.

She tries to call Henry again in Berwick.

Straight to messenger.

She stands looking out at the Charles Bridge. Apparently the arguments about the ongoing repairs still alive.

Her mobile purrs.

She listens.

Says nothing.

Closes the phone.

She and Otka know how to disappear, they grew up doing it. But Xavi is hopeless. No matter the strength in his limbs and a heart like a lion, he's easily fooled – believes the best of everybody, even when it's staring him in the face.

What was it some Russian said in the revolution?

Anyway, it's hardly likely anyone could find them here, only Otka worked in the house and she pretended not to have much English and the documents she gave the catering firm were all fake and now non-existent.

But all the same the risks were still taken and they deserved their rewards . . . and then she thought of that Italian guy. Hadn't used him since the Florence job.

So she finds his number, calls it and leaves a message.

* * *

'Bloody interfering busybodies,' growled Walker.

He and Gill are sitting in his car outside Kelso Police station. It's shut, of course, at the moment, because the staff have been cut to the bone. Most work done on computers now and that can be done anywhere.

Gill assumes he's talking about the previous DI, and her brother, aided and abetted by another ex-cop, called Becket . . . as well as that weird computer guy who rarely goes anywhere and dresses like a late 90s female punk.

Saying anything about that is pointless and anyway she's still angry at her father bloody dying on her without a single word spoken. No letter. Not even a 'sorry'.

She's been told by the solicitor in Montrose of all places . . . as down and out dead place you could ever find, even in Fife, ffs . . . that he can't send her a copy or read the will out over the phone, even though he's said she's the only beneficiary, but still insists she's got to go to his office . . . 'at her convenience'!

And now she's supposed to deal with these rich folk who've been robbed of stuff they probably robbed from someone else centuries ago . . . alongside this black dude who doesn't seem to understand he's been shelved.

'Well,' she says, thinking all that anger has just dissipated because she's said it to herself and in any case she's thinking what the old bastard might have left her. The cottage belongs to the estate and probably his dog as well. She doubts he'd got any savings or a funeral insurance policy, so she'll probably have to pay for that. The Vikings had the best idea - burn the 'buggers', which is exactly what she's decided to do. Not in the Viking manner, of course.

'What? says Walker frowning at her.

'Oh, did I just say that out loud?' she mumbles.

'Something about Vikings?' he asks.

'Ah, yes, just thinking about my dad's funeral . . .'

He keeps looking at her.

'No, not in a boat . . . although he did have one, on the lochan.'

'I'm not sure you can do that anyway nowadays . . . although you can take him out and dump him into the sea . . . I think?'

She nearly laughs.

'A bit repetitive since he drowned himself,' she says.

Walker looks at her again.

'You know you can have compassionate leave don't you?' he asks.

She shakes her head.

'No, I don't think so . . . I might need a day off for the funeral and go to Montrose for the reading of the will.'

Walker waits to see if there's anything else, thinking comforting a lost daughter might be out of his empathy range, especially as it seems her main response is some sort of internal anger.

'Will that be soon?' seems the only safe question.

She shrugs.

'When I get round to it . . .'

This difficult conversation is thankfully interrupted by Walker's phone vibrating.

He listens.

'Where?'

He listens again, but then puts his phone to his chest.

'Ladykirk?'

Gill frowns and then nods, recalling an old kirk up above Norham.

'Yes,' he says to his phone and then listens.

For some time.

'I see, so we're claiming it, because I was the last person to contact him . . .' shaking his head at Gill.

There's a lot more said, but he only says 'OK', 'alright' and 'yes sir' numerous times, until he ends the call.

Gill waits, she can see he's controlling his temper.

'So,' he says. 'An old man, a bit of a dealer in 'historical items' has been found dead in Berwick . . . which you know is in England, but the Northumberland police have 'agreed for us to liaise with them' , to see if it might may be connected to the robbery at the big house.'

Gill frowns.

'How connected?'

'Photos found of the items stolen from there.'

'Oh.'

He gets a message, sighs and turns on the engine.

'House on the battlements apparently, I've sent you the details.'

She brings the message up on her phone and scrolls down to the photographs.

'I see, do you know Berwick?'

He shakes his head.

'Never been.'

'Ah, well . . . then you're in for a historical treat or how the English tried to protect themselves from us barbarians.'

'Not my lot, I doubt,' he laughs.

*   *   *

Although Amelia was a bit put out to find two more waifs and strays Magda's brought to the house, she tells herself to remember how grateful she was when she and her children were in the same position and then when she hears what's happened to Catherine and her two daughters, she's filled with anger all over again.

So sheets and duvets are quickly rescued from the upstairs cupboards and the windows opened to air the rooms, before Amelia takes charge of the older girls getting dinner on the way whilst Magda, Helena and Catherine have drinks on the terrace.

But then Catherine's mobile is burbling and although she hesitates, she answers it and goes to the far end.

Magda can tell she's listening rather than speaking and it's a long call, but when it's finished she sees that she's crying.

She goes over and puts her arms around her until she stops.

Then listens to what he's said.

So when Amelia arrives with a tray of drinks and nibbles, she puts them down and frowns at Helena, who shrugs.

'Husband. I think?' she murmurs.

Then Magda brings Catherine over and tells them what her husband has said.

'He's sending people who will find the burglars and 'deal with them',' she says.

Amelia frowns.

'I thought the police were 'dealing' with it?'

Catherine shakes her head.

'It's not the loss of the things that were stolen, he's angry that someone had the temerity to steal anything from him . . . which means the people who he's sending will . . . kill them . . .'

Whilst Amelia and Helena have been in situations involving excessive violence, they can't help but be astounded.

No-one can speak for a few moments.

'So . . .' murmurs Amelia, 'what do we do?'

*   *   *

Eventually I manage to crawl and slither over the rocks and find a bush to rest behind.

There are no other people and the path this side is faint.

In the distance I can see smoke from a chimney being waved about by the wind, which makes me shiver.

The thought of a fire roasting a haunch of beef makes my mouth water, although I've more chance of catching a fish.

Then it dawns on me that I'm on the wrong side of the river, which means anyone I meet is likely to be Scots, who'll certainly kill me without thinking.

But then I think of the English, after all it was them that imprisoned me on this side . . . and then that reminds me of that evil man who told them to do it and they were even worse, Frenchies, pirates the lot of them.

So . . . what to do?

If my memory saves me right, Berwick is a good ten miles away from Norham and that's on the road the other side.

Looking at the sun, which is sinking way upstream, it would be better to find somewhere to rest for the night.

CHAPTER SIX

URSULA

You'd think given the multiplying ghosts back at our house by the river – I nearly called it 'home'? – that I'd not be worried about ghosts elsewhere . . . but Berwick makes me uneasy.

As we make our way through the town, I tell myself I'm hardly likely to see any in this bright sunlight, but I become more and more aware of figures just out of the corner of my eye and when I look quickly to catch them they turn out to be real people or no-one at all.

Becket seems to know where she's going and as usual takes a route meant to flummox anyone following us. Just her ingrained self-protection at work.

But it doesn't take too long for us to come out at a huge square with a couple of churches side by side.

She ignores the newer of the two and crosses between the cars to the one in the corner calling itself the Holy Trinity.

Again she surprises me by wandering around looking at gravestones.

'So it seems this wasn't here until the end of the eighteenth century,' she says pointing at one, which despite its age I can see clearly that Cornelius Nisbet was interred in 1798. Not my period, as Ellie would say.

Now she's taking a photo and sending it to Ziggy.

'Just to keep the bugger on his toes,' she murmurs with a sly smile.

The only event that comes to mind from my limited historical knowledge is that was around the time of the

French revolution . . . which Ziggy says they 'stuck to, not like us'? Not sure what he meant by that but no use asking him to clarify.

So now we're going up a sloping path to a gate to get onto the walls, but I'm more interested in the big gate which opens onto a huge square – 'the Barracks' . . . and wondering whether anyone's still stationed there . . . still needing to keep them Scotties back?

Now Janet's vanished and I walk fast to get through the gate and then find her standing higher up looking out to sea.

There's a vast expanse of mud and water filling the estuary this side of a long seawall.

And now she's off again, striding along as though she's going to a meeting . . . which we are . . . although it's not what I was expecting.

*   *   *

Walker and Gill are frustrated to find the ex-soldier and his weird 'partner' already at the police station in Berwick and even worse to find them already in the Inspector's office.

So they get a DS, who tells them the story.

'Looks like the burglars were expecting more than they could find, although the safe was open and quite expensive stuff left as though as they'd been disturbed.'

'Why do you think that?' asks Walker.

The Inspector shrugs.

'Why would you leave what you'd come for?'

'What about cameras?' asks Gill impatiently which gets her a smug shake off his head.

'Nothing,' he adds, 'we're not in the middle of Manchester here and there's no sign of a forced entrance. Nothing on the cameras in the vicinity.'

'Nothing in the house?' she continues.

'Didn't appear to have been turned on, nothing on the tape.'

Walker stares at him thinking 'when's the cooperation going to start', but Gill has even less patience.

'So why kill him?'

Again the man shrugs.

Fortunately the door opens before Gill can express the rage bursting inside her head.

It's the Inspector who appears and he apologises for keeping them waiting and asks them to come into his office.

They are just in time to see the disappearing figures of the ex-soldier and his 'partner'.

The frustration levels do get less, but when they leave half an hour later, Gill is still spitting feathers.

Without discussion they make their way to the house, which turns out to be the middle of three houses, all looking as though no-one's living in them. No curtains in the first two and the third has closed shutters on the ground and first floors.

'So, they think this is just an interrupted burglary and not likely to be anyone from Berwick?' she rasps.

'Yeh . . . and they're not interested in connecting it with the burglary at the big house outside Jedburgh . . . 'there's no evidence that he had received anything that's on the missing list . . . at best a wrong guess from the burglars."

Gill is staring out a sea.

'But . . . what if the mad husband sent someone to check him out.'

Walker sighs and then shrugs.

He makes a call to Tomasz, who says that they're waiting by the big gun round the corner.

But it's not just Tomasz, it's Becket and even that weird woman who doesn't speak as well.

Walker shakes hands with Tomasz and Becket, but Gill can only manage a nod, whilst Imelda is looking out to sea and ignores them.

'So what d'you think?' asks Walker.

Tomasz smiles, a cold grimace.

'Why would someone kill the old guy and not take anything.'

Walker shrugs.

'Where I come from people get killed for a glance at a girl or you say Man U are crap.'

'Did any of the Berwick 'polis' suggest any other motive?' asks Becket.

'Not really, I think they think whoever it was were disturbed and left without taking anything . . . but without a list of items it's difficult to say what might be missing . . . it's not as if they trashed the place,' says Tomasz.

'Have they managed to contact anyone else like his friends, business partners . . . his bank?'

Tomasz shrugs again.

'They didn't tell me.'

Gill snorts.

'If this is the best the English police can do I think they're probably in with the gang!'

Walker sighs.

'All we can do is contact the man's insurance company and see if they've got a list.'

Tomasz makes a face.

'I think the Berwick police are on to that and not keen on sharing . . . but I'm now wondering if he has family or friends who might know what's missing.'

Which is the moment a young woman and a dog come round the corner.

Walker and Gill can't believe it.

This gang getting in the way is becoming ridiculous.

Briefest greetings over and done with, they share their thoughts and investigations, which ends with Ellie contacting

Ziggy, who's on the case and has come up with a relative – a sister who lives down by the estuary only five minutes' walk away.

*   *   *

Voudra is feeling sorry for herself.

She's fallen from greater heights before but this time she landed awkwardly. Nothing broken, but a seriously bruised shoulder, meaning they had to cancel Lyon. So doing her usual thing when she's injured: being miserable and sullen, not even worth asking how she is, unless you wanted a barrage of expletives in various languages telling you to 'go away' etcetera.

So they then decided to return to the UK to keep tabs on the investigation in Scotland.

Not much in the news and nothing in the English papers, so staying in their Saltburn house is well out of the way.

Xavi not sure what to do between her and a short tempered Otka, who is spending most of the time online. So he takes the next-door old lady's dog for long walks on the beach and in the woods.

Otka's seen a short piece in the local press about the robbery, but nothing since, so now trying to access police conversations without much success.

But the most worrying thing is nothing from Henry. Not answering his phone, which is unheard of, he's always on his phone.

So she thinks it's worth a risk contacting one of the local rags pretending to be a national reporter wanting to get an update.

'Just wondering if there's any developments in the robbery from the big house near Jedburgh?' she asks, but three calls later she gives up.

Stands looking out at the sea.

Xavi arrives quietly with a mug of coffee, puts it down on the table and turns to creep back out.

'Fancy a drive, Xavs?'

He turns and risks a smile, thinking he'll get a barrage of abuse for even thinking that would be alright.

But no, it's a genuine invitation and two hours or so later, they're turning off the AI into Berwick.

They park up near two churches and Otka goes straight towards the older one and disappears. Xavi doesn't do churches, and graveyards never, so he waits, but then remembering Otka's fascination for them and how long she can be, he eventually gets out and wanders over to the gate into the Barracks.

They've been here quite a few times when they were checking out some of the bigger houses on the walls, but most of them looked too difficult, expensive alarms systems likely and Otka preferred single properties in the countryside.

She taps him on the shoulder, having crept up behind him silently as usual, like a ghost.

'Thinking of joining up, Xavs?' she grins.

He shakes his head.

'Let's go down to the little beach,' she murmurs, 'and then I'll take you out for lunch.'

She sets off and he follows, 'like a dog' he thinks, but if she's offering to buy him lunch then that generally means something to follow on . . . and no Voudra to share it with.

So, he follows her through a tunnel beneath the wall and they come out on the side of the estuary, which today is full of water, instead of the mud he's usually seen.

There's a row of houses on the left and some old folk sitting out in the sunshine.

They smile and say hello as they pass and continue to the end, where they come to the hidden beach beyond the sea wall.

Both of them having been born hundreds of miles away from any sea, they are both awed and slightly fearful of the waves, but today they're quietly flopping onto the shingle and so they take off their shoes and socks and wander along the shoreline.

They only meet one person, a man with a daft dog, who delights in chasing after sticks and running into the waves to fetch them.

But now Otka is on the phone.

Finishes and frowns.

Xavi waits.

'He's still not answering,' she whispers. 'I think we'll risk a visit . . . well, a walk past.'

So, they walk back up towards the wall, but as they reach the old folk sitting out they see there's a couple of younger people talking to them.

Otka whispers 'keep going' and they pass without speaking.

Through the tunnel and up onto the wall.

Otka stops and looks down at the old folk talking to the couple.

'*Politciya*,' she whispers.

Xavi stares at them, but knows she has an acute antenna for them. The black guy just looks badly dressed to him, but the woman looks like she can handle herself.

She takes her phone out and tries Henry again, no answer, so they wander along the front and back. Nothing to see, but now she takes him down to the back street and there they see the police tapes and a uniform standing at the door.

Before he can think of making for the nearest exit, she's walking up to the officer on guard and flashes a reporter's card at him.

The officer just waves her away and so she gracefully carries on. He follows, his heart beating like a train.

Five minutes later they're sitting in the car. Otka's staring through the windscreen, he can almost hear her brain whirring.

'Something's happened to Henry,' she whispers, 'but I doubt he's ever told anyone about us.'

He looks at her, her face is blank, not worried, but then he knows that's worrying . . . he knows what she's capable of doing . . . but then she turns and smiles at him.

'In any case we've never met so he couldn't tell them very much . . . and as we only communicate via different post restante addresses every time . . .'

Xavi is still frowning.

'But . . .

She sighs.

'You're right, I've no idea.'

*   *   *

Dawn comes early on this side of the river.

A red sun promising rain.

I wake with a growing pain in my belly. I need to eat something.

I crawl out from under the overhang and look around.

Even in this light I can see the black jewels hanging in a bramble bush, which I hadn't noticed last night, so I can take away the raw hunger with a few mouthfuls, washed down by some water from a rivulet going down to the river.

And then I spy the boots.

Some angel looking after me.

They're made with a leather so smooth and the insides are furred. There's also laces to tie them tight.

But first I need to clean my feet which are covered in dirt and dried blood, so I crawl down to the river.

It's only when I've finished and sit there waiting for my feet to dry that I see the fishing line hanging from a branch over the river.

Forgetting my feet I clamber over and see that it's just a few twists round the branch and I can undo it.

And lo and behold there's a hook on the end and on the hook is a fish.

'Jesu save me!!' I cry.

So soon I get a little fire going and cook the fish and eat it.

'Thanks be to God' I murmur.

But now the sun has risen high above the trees on the other side of the river, so I collect my little possessions including the line, and set off.

It's maybe an hour before I see a bridge in the distance, which puzzles me. I didn't think there was one between Norham and Berwick.

Both sides of the river have steep banks with lots of trees, although on this side I can see a meadow further along which will be easier walking.

The other thing that worries me is not seeing anyone else.

The meadow is closely cropped which suggests that there might be cattle or sheep, but there's no trace of them.

But, what's worrying me now is the bridge . . . and the occasional noise of a cart rattling along, but a strange whirring noise and it's gone as soon as I hear it.

So now I get to the edge of the meadow and I can see the bridge clearly, even though the sky has clouded over and rain is in the air.

Huge towers on both sides of the river with lines attached to hold it up.

I can't see any soldiers on either side, which is unbelievable. In fact there are no folk at all.

I get nearer, clambering about next to a fence below the trees until I get to the bridge.

Still no soldiers.

No people?

It's unreal!

I climb to the road and look across the bridge. No guards. No . . . there is! One man sitting looking like he's staring at me.

But then I hear a rumbling and see movement high up on the other side. A monster rushing down the hill.

In a panic I dash across the road and hunker down behind a bush.

The monster comes hurtling across the bridge, but doesn't stop, just carries on and disappears.

I'm shaking like a feather; I've wet myself and can feel the warmth in my groin.

I now realise there's a house on this side, so I creep along a hedge and peep over. But I can see it's not inhabited; the roof has fallen in and there's brambles and grasses inside.

So I carry on as fast as I can go until I've put half a league behind me.

There are no other monsters or any houses or people to be seen, so eventually I find cover under a cliff and stop.

My heart is still racing and my head is singing with fear.

What's happening? Is this hell? Am I dead?

CHAPTER SEVEN

Louisa insists on going to Henry's solicitor, who to be honest isn't that surprised to see her.

'I was going to phone you,' he murmurs, as she and Fletcher are ushered into his office.

'This is my friend, Michael . . . he's a 'retired detective',' she says, making it sound rather disreputable, which he has to agree he was.

'So what do you know?' she demands, trying not to be imperious, but failing.

The solicitor, who's called Angus Maxwell, nods at him and sighs.

'Not a lot to be honest . . . a break-in which went wrong, burglars left without taking anything, the police think he may have disturbed them . . .'

Louisa frowns.

'How can they know that?'

'The safe wasn't opened and there was no sign of things missing.'

Louisa stares at him waiting for more.

He shrugs.

'We know he's dead but did they say how?' ask Fletcher.

'Blow to the head, I think . . . it would have been instantaneous they said.'

Louisa sighs.

'Sounds a bit odd, who or what disturbed them . . . apart from Henry?'

Maxwell shrugs.

'No idea.'

The room fills with silence, motes in the sun coming through the window.

'Can we have a look?' asks Fletcher.

Maxwell shrugs.

'You could ask . . . after all Louisa is the executor.'

Fletcher looks back at her.

'You don't need to look at me like that, he was John's best man at our wedding,' she rasps.

Fletcher shrugs, he wasn't there obviously, while Maxwell nods his head.

Louisa is frowning at Fletcher, but now stands up.

'Well, if you give me the keys we can go now . . . no point in waiting as we're here already.'

So ten minutes later they're standing in the front room, which is full of sunshine now that Fletcher's pulled back the curtains.

'Fantastic view,' he murmurs, looking out at the estuary, which is full of dark water.

Louisa has found the key which opens his desk drawer and pulls out a much-scuffed ledger.

'He was a meticulous man was Henry, not like some people I know,' she says looking over her glasses at him.

'Ah well, some people have so little they don't need a list,' he laughs and then realises that's maybe a bit sad . . . he's used to not staying anywhere long or with anyone either . . . except, he frowns, wondering how long he's managed to stay with Louisa or more pertinently, how long she's allowed him to stay.

She shakes her head.

But then she carefully goes from room to room ticking off what's on the list and then, using the key she got from the solicitor, opens the safe to check out the latest items.

'That's strange,' she says, holding a slip of paper which was in the between the last pages.

She stares at it for a few moments and then shows it to him.

It's obviously some sort of code which doesn't immediately mean much to either of them.

'1814-1317-1956-72?' he murmurs.

She looks at him over her glasses.

'Any ideas?' she demands, but he can only shake his head.

'Well, whatever it means, it doesn't seem to have interested the would-be burglars.'

Fletcher sighs.

'So what happens next?'

'Maxwell will arrange for a will reading and then something will have to be done about the house . . . and contents.'

Fletcher looks out the window again, but shivers.

'Well, the view is wonderful, but . . . to be honest it feels cold . . . not lived in for some time . . .'

Louisa stares at him.

'Not usual for you to 'feel' something?' she asks.

He shrugs, it's not the first house he's entered to find someone dead, although it's not the absence of the body . . . it just feels empty . . . not lived in . . . 'like a mortuary' he says out loud.

Louisa shakes her head, but then shivers.

'Come on,' she says brusquely, 'we've things to do.'

With that she sets off, her heels clicking on the marble floor . . . so Fletcher takes one last look at the view and follows on.

*   *   *

Tomasz has had a phone call.

So now they're on their way back home.

Imelda has seen the closed face, so no words are spoken.

Back at the house there's a sombre mood, Catherine has stopped crying, but now sits looking out the window not wanting to talk.

Magda ushers Tomasz out onto the balcony, which is where all serious conversations happen in their family.

'She's had three phone calls from that vile man, so I've taken her phone . . . and actually I think she was relieved . . . and I've not answered it since . . . although fortunately it tells me where he's phoning from.'

Tomasz waits.

'Well, the first ones were from Singapore, but the latest was from a plane over the Pacific Ocean, so Catherine thinks he'll be heading for Los Angeles.'

Tomasz takes a slug of his coffee.

'What about the daughter?'

Magda shakes her head.

'Not sure . . . I haven't taken her phone, but she doesn't seem to be using it.'

Tomasz frowns.

'I thought they were on their phones all the time?'

Magda sighs.

'In my experience, family problems cause all sorts of responses . . . few of them logical.'

Tomasz smiles.

'I'm assuming you're talking professionally . . . not about us!'

She grins.

'Oh, no, we're very predictable!'

They both laugh.

Helena has come out to see what they're up to and is puzzled by their laughter.

They can't help feeling caught out, which she was always able to do when they'd done something wrong.

'So what have you two decided to do about this . . .' but then gave up and shrugged her shoulders, not able to find the English word for this 'situation'.

'Not sure, mumya,' says Magda.

Helena stares at Tomasz.

He shrugs.

'He's high up above the Pacific Ocean, even I can't get to him there.'

Helena doesn't smile.

'Well, you'd better have your gun ready before he comes here.'

He shakes his head.

*　　　*　　　*

Walker's getting that bad feeling when a case seems to be slipping away from him.

It's never easy to put a finger on why or how this happens, but he's come to recognise the symptoms.

First, there's no indication why the murder's happened. Someone killed the guy but didn't seem to have taken anything when there was plenty to take. Secondly, and this is becoming a fixture in the Borders, there's all these interfering would be detectives getting under his feet.

The only lead seems to be talking to the victim's sister, who also lives in the town – 'outwith' the walls as the solicitor puts it.

Gill knows how to get to the house but it means going under the wall, through a narrow gateway, which gives way to the expanse of water filling the estuary.

It's only a few houses down and they find the woman sitting outside in the sunshine.

They're taken indoors and tea and biscuits are organised, whether they want them or not.

So they're sitting on low settees both feeling awkward and in fact Gill is now standing up, looking out the window.

Walker always feels uneasy when visiting grieving relatives, although to be honest this woman doesn't seem to be doing that . . . which might be worse.

'It's alright,' she says, as though she's reading his mind, 'my brother and I haven't spoken for forty years, ever since he got the house and I got a couple of paintings when our father died, who thought young ladies should look for a husband instead.'

Walker can't help but look at the painting over the fireplace.

'No, I had to sell them,' she says with a smile. 'Weird old Lowry's anyway . . . him and his 'stick' people . . . must have had something wrong with his eyes, I think.'

Walker is now totally lost. Lowry? 'Stick' people?

'Anyway, what do you want to know? I can't imagine I can be any help . . . like I said, I've only caught sight of him in the town

83

occasionally, but I suspect that was because he didn't get out much . . . rather solitary, like his father.'

Walker is getting a headache but is saved by Gill.

'So, you wouldn't know if he had any enemies or people he'd upset?' she asks as she turns round.

The sister shrugs.

'Not a clue.'

This is so finite, that Walker is thinking they may as well go.

'Well, can you think of anyone who might have known him better?' Gill asks.

The old lady smiles.

'I guess old Peacham would be your best bet. He runs the art shop in town just off the High Street. I think they've always been thick as thieves, went to the same posh school, where they were taught they were above everyone else.'

Walker can't remember what else was said but was mightily relieved to be back out on the street and into the fresh air.

The day didn't get any better at the art shop, because the other posh boy was away, leaving a rather unhelpful young woman to mind the shop and so they decided to head back 'home', Walker saying he'd just have to get in touch with the Super and let him decide what to do next.

URSULA

'Well, that's a lot of coming and going . . . without any outcomes,' as my old boss used to say, indicating to one and all that it wasn't his fault and what were they going to do about it?

I'd never been to Berwick before, but for some reason I quite like it. 'Fresh air and fun' as old Stanley Holloway told it.

Janet's fed up for the same reasons. She's never really stopped thinking she would do a lot better than *anybody finding answers, although she grudgingly admitted once that Fletcher wasn't 'half bad at it'.*

And now he's been whisked away by Louisa after they'd been to see the solicitor, because apparently she's the person the dead man had made his executor, which means we're here at a loose end now, which is not Janet's favourite occupation.

But then she gets a message from Ziggy.

'What code?' she asks.

'How did you get it from her?'

'I see . . . so . . .'

She pauses again.

'Oh . . . have you told . . ?

There's then a lot more words from him before she cuts the call.

I wait, watching her mind ticking over.

She's staring out at the estuary.

Then she remembers I'm standing next to her.

'Apparently some of the stolen articles include a ruby necklace given to the family by Mary Queen of Scots and two glass bowls from Elizabeth the First.'

I stare at her trying to imagine how much they would be worth now . . . and then remembering that Elizabeth had Mary executed . . . and then wondering why the family managed to have them.

But Janet's shaking her head.

'Ziggy says they'd be worth enormous sums of money but very difficult to sell, even though there are plenty of rich people who would be willing to bid for them.'

*　　　*　　　*

Otka is standing at the railing on a promenade.

She's told Xavi to drive them here so that she can figure out what to do next.

He's sitting outside a café, trying to drink a rather insipid cup of coffee, which is rapidly getting cold in the breeze.

He was a bit puzzled when they'd crossed the bridge to go south, thinking they're going home, but then she told him to make a left turn and they ended up at a dreary out of season seaside place called Spittal. He knows that asking her what she's thinking will only get him a glare, so he's learnt to be patient and he knows solving problems is what she does best.

But now she's on the phone.

Walking backwards and forwards.

She stops.

Shakes her head and ends the call.

He waits.

She shakes her head again and then comes back to sit with him.

'Voudra says the police are treating it as a robbery which went wrong, but they don't seem to have any leads and there's no mention of the necklace or the glass vases . . . so . . .'

Xavi waits.

'Apparently they think Henry had a heart attack, rather than been killed by the burglars . . .'

He frowns, thinking Henry was in his sixties, but he didn't seem to be unfit, especially as Voudra said he walked the walls every day and apparently was a fine 'badminton player', a game which he'd never seen or played.

Otka looks at him . . . always a bit scary . . . one green, one blue eye.

'Let's go find a place to stay, see what happens. I'll get Voudra to see if she can hack the police investigations, I'm not sure how the different forces manage to cooperate, although, however they do it there'll be a lot of traffic online and phones I imagine.'

Xavi's looking at his own phone.

'Where do you want to be - here or back in Berwick?'

She shrugs.

'Better to be close to the police who are dealing with it, I think . . . and I don't want to be here, it's dreary and full of dog walkers.'

*   *   *

I don't manage to go very far after that scare at the bridge.

But as the sun is sinking under the clouds upstream, I need somewhere better to hide for the night and I can see there's a lot of trees further along, so I set off.

It's not far and I find a ledge a few feet above the shingle where there are more bramble bushes and then I notice that the hillside is riddled with rabbit holes.

So remembering how the forester who lived not far from my mother's house, who always had a few rabbits hanging from his porch and how he showed me how to catch them, I set a trap and wait patiently.

As the sun went down they started to come out and sure enough one of them was caught.

Having assuaged my hunger, I kept the fire burning for comfort's sake and to give me some light to clean the skin, which I think might make a little covering for my bald pate.

So I was half sleep when the noise began.

At first I couldn't work out where it was coming from, but then the sky was filled with lightning and explosions. Not as loud as cannons, but then I saw the rockets flying and dropping into the river, which made me think of the wonderful evenings back on my master's estate.

Then the huge noise of a band, louder than anything I've ever heard, blasting out strange music, but also someone singing, so loud I thought he must be really close.

I crept out to look up the hillside and was astonished at the brightness of the lights, some of them changing colours as I watched.

I crept back, shivering, wondering how close they must be, but could only huddle back as far as I could on the ledge.

I've heard rumours of how savage and cruel the Scots can be, roasting poor captives alive before eating them . . . and other evil, bestial pursuits.

The weird music seemed to go on forever, but eventually there was a barrage of enormous explosions and some loud singing, which gradually finished with hundreds of bursts of lightning in the sky and lots of cheering.

I waited to see if there was any more but eventually there was silence and I huddled down to try and get some sleep.

CHAPTER EIGHT

Walker is thinking of finding himself a B&B in Berwick even though Superintendent McGregor tells him to leave it to the fraud squad, who he says have got some 'whispers'.

Gill has gone up north for the reading of her father's will, so he's being shadowed by DS Rossi, who always makes him feel awkward. His unreadable dark eyes might mean he's awestruck by this senior officer's methods or more likely he's not worked with a black officer before.

Well, going door to door in the area around the murdered man's house didn't seem outside of basic police procedure, even though he strictly didn't have the authority to do it.

And it was a waste of time.

Both the big houses either side are unoccupied. One because it was being sold and the other because the owners were in the Caribbean . . . which he had to admit seemed a very good idea indeed . . . if only.

'So . . .' he murmurs to Rossi as they stand in one of the big front rooms which has great views of the estuary, which isn't as lovely as one might have thought. Even in the bright sunshine it's a huge expanse of rather evil looking mud and sluggish water.

Rossi waits impassively.

'I just don't get it,' growls Walker.

Rossi's eyes go bigger.

'The burglars get in but this old guy has a heart attack and dies or he's already had it and is lying on the floor?'

Rossi manages a shrug.

'Either way . . . ' he demands, ' why didn't they take anything?'

'Maybe they did . . . but it wasn't insured . . . or he'd not had time to arrange that?' Rossi offers.

They'd been to the art shop, but frustrated again because the owner was away, not back until the end of the week.

So they've now come down and found a YHA café, which seems to be empty.

'My wife always comes here . . .' murmurs Rossi apologetically, as though they ought to be going to an Italian one.

Walker frowns again.

'What if McGregor's right and the whole thing is an insurance scam?'

Rossi stares at him.

'You mean the owners? Lady Catherine?'

Walker shakes his head.

'More likely the husband . . . although I suspect she married him after her first husband died and had to pay the death duties.'

Rossi shakes his head.

But Walker ploughs on this particular furrow.

'So who do we contact?'

Rossi frowns.

'Their solicitors?'

Walker stands up.

'So let's get back to Scotland and find out.'

Rossi hardly gets time to drink his coffee, as Walker is out the door and striding away.

So it's on the way back that Walker's on his phone tracking down who he needs talk to . . . which turns out to be big firm in Edinburgh, although they have a small office in Jedburgh, so that's where they're heading.

It's only when they're nearly there that Rossi wonders if they ought to be contacting the wife.

'You're right,' says Walker, 'and we know where she's been hijacked to, don't we?'

Again Rossi can only nod but thinking that's not going to easy either.

*   *   *

The 'hijackers' have been able to lift a little of the spirits of the wife and daughter and this has been helped by the arrival of her elder sister, Mary, who seems a more composed presence.

Walker and Rossi can't help but feeling both outnumbered and out-'classed' in this situation, partly by the house itself, so they accept the enforced welcome led by Magda and Tomasz's mother.

So, it's a good half hour before they get round to the awkward questioning.

Even so, Walker ditches his usual blunt method which just adds to his difficulties and knowing that he won't get any help for Rossi. How much he wishes Gill was here, she'd be straight in with her no-nonsense approach.

Eventually, he manages to ask to speak to the wife on her own and even then gives in to Magda staying with her.

And then . . . where to start?

The silence thickens making it even harder.

Until it's Magda who breaks the tension.

'I think Catherine is finding this very difficult, Inspector . . . because . . . well, her husband has . . . is . . . a very angry man.'

Walker nods his head and waits, thinking 'let her go on'.

Magda squeezes Catherine's hand.

'Well, to be blunt, he's furious and . . . we think he's . . . taking measures to . . . find the culprits . . .'

Walker looks from one to the other and frowns.

'What sort of measures?' he asks.

'Well,' says Magda, looking at Catherine who makes a small nod of her head, whilst looking away through the window.

'I suppose 'private' . . . investigators?'

Walker shakes his head.

'That's not a good idea . . .'

Now Catherine looks directly at him, with a steely gaze.

'You've no idea, Inspector, what he's capable of when he gets angry . . . and he is very, very angry about this.'

Walker frowns, wondering what that might mean.

'He's been violent to both Catherine and her children.'

Walker stares at Magda, but can't help glancing at Rossi, who seems dumbstruck.

'Well . . .' he says trying to calm the atmosphere, 'as I understand it, he's not actually in the country yet? Singapore?'

Catherine shakes her head.

'No, he's flying to Los Angeles.'

Rossi frowns.

'Well, even that's many hours away.'

Magda can't stand this.

'Don't you understand, Inspector . . . this man is very rich, and powerful, and isn't used to people stealing from him . . . so he's taking it as a serious affront to his . . .'

She can't finish the sentence because Catherine is weeping . . . and shaking.

Walker waits, his head buzzing, partly worrying what his superiors know about this and also getting angry that he might be sidelined if it's gets more 'difficult'.

But now Catherine finds some Border family steel.

'He's a proud man and is taking this as an insult to his 'masculinity' . . . and I wish I'd never let myself be fooled by his false . . . '

She stands up and goes to the window.

Magda is still glaring at Walker, who now nods his understanding and stands up.

'Don't worry, I'll be explaining to my superiors how . . . dangerous this situation is becoming.'

He beckons to Magda that he'll go to talk to Tomasz.

Stepping back into the main room, he nods at Tomasz and the two of them go out onto the balcony.

'You get the picture?' demands Tomasz.

Walker nods.

Tomasz waits, wondering why he's stalling.

Walker sighs.

'I looked you up,' he murmurs and gives him a sly smile.

Tomasz frowns.

'Very impressive . . . and actually quite scary.'

Tomasz can only look away.

Walker pulls out his cigarettes and lights one up.

'I realise I'd be wasting my breath telling you to leave it to us . . .' he murmurs.

Tomasz can't help but smile but then his face goes stern.

'If what I've found out about this 'man', he's perfectly capable of paying for the best and that he'll also know all about me . . . so I would expect a small army.'

'And more worryingly , he doesn't have to be here . . . does he?' says Walker, looking across at the far hillside.

Tomasz smiles.

'I could do it, but there's very few others could and you'd need my rifle, there's only one like it.'

Walker stares at him.

'Really? How far is it?'

Tomasz's face is blank, like he's back in the field.

'As long as she's inside, she's safe, but . . .'

Walker waits.

But then Tomasz whispers.

'I'd find him, wherever he tries to hide.'

Walker stares at him again and shivers, he's never heard such cold words spoken.

They both stand waiting.

But it's Magda who breaks the silence.

'The husband is trying to call Catherine,' she tells them.

Walker nods and goes back into the room and asks to take over the call, but it's gone dead.

He turns to look at the wife, but she's been comforted by Helena.

He gives Tomasz a look and nods towards the door.

In the hall he promises to contact his superiors, explain the danger that the family are in and get them to arrange some strong protection as soon as possible.

Tomasz stares at him, but eventually nods.

Outside Walker tells Rossi to drive, but as soon as they're along the valley he tells him to pull in, so he can make the phone call.

And afterwards he has to get out of the car and scream at the trees . . . which doesn't bother them one bit, although it frightens the life out of Rossi.

*   *   *

As the only people who are required at the reading of the will are Louisa and Henry's sister, the solicitor agrees to get it over with.

And it's very brief and rather awkward.

He'd secretly bought the two Lowry's that his sister sold years ago and now he bequeaths them to her again, which thankfully just makes her laugh, but then the solicitor tells her how much they're now worth, which makes her gasp . . . and then he tells her that the town council are very interested in buying them, so that seems to be a happy solution.

Louisa is also bequeathed any one piece for being 'a faithful friend' which makes her squirm, thinking of all the times she's come to Berwick without seeing him . . . because he was such a terrible bore.

The rest of his collection and the house are to be sold at auction and the proceeds to be given to ongoing repairs to the Walls.

So Louisa shakes hands with the solicitor and the sister and they both walk along to take one last look at the house and for the sister to rescue the Lowry's.

Fletcher has been summoned to carry them to the sister's house, but then they notice the two photos clipped onto the back of one of them.

Louisa frowns as she looks at them and then gasps.

'I think those are two of the items stolen from Catherine!'

She shows them to Fletcher, who shakes his head.

'Really?' he asks, 'does that mean he bought them?'

Louisa shakes her head.

'No, I think he had been asked to find a buyer and that's why he was killed.'

Fletcher frowns.

'So Henry didn't actually have them here?'

Louisa shakes her head.

'I doubt it and he would know he would never be able to sell them . . . unless . . .'

'Unless?' Fletcher repeats.

Louisa stares at him.

'Do you have any idea how much they would be worth?'

He shrugs.

'Thousands?'

She laughs.

'You 'daft apeth'!

He stares at her.

'Millions!!' she whispers . . . which is when Ellie appears at the window, first with a big grin and then a frown. She indicates she's going to the door.

Fletcher sets off, still not believing a necklace and a couple of fancy jars can be worth millions?

He's only half-way there when Louisa shouts at him: 'don't' let her bring the dog in! Henry hated them!"

He opens the door and obediently repeats Louisa's order, which always annoys Ellie.

'The man's dead for heaven's sake,' she mutters, but then sees the photographs in his hand.

'Aha,' she grins and shows him the same pictures on her mobile screen. 'Snap!'

So ten minutes later they're sitting outside Henry's sister's house, who they now know is called Joan.

She brings out a tray of coffee, four glasses and a bottle of Armagnac.

Rollo is trying to be not too excited meeting a smaller version of himself, although Doodie is considerably older as well.

'So,' says Joan, 'what excitement!' and then looks at the astonished faces.

'Oh, I'm sorry, I suppose I ought to be sad . . . we've not even buried him yet.'

Again this is a bit awkward and she shrugs.

'Always putting my foot in it . . . sorry.'

The other three wave it away and everyone tucks into the madeira cake which next appeared.

But then Louisa asks how Ellie found the photos.

She makes a face: 'Who do you think?'

Fletcher grins.

'Mr Hook, I presume.'

Louisa shakes her head.

'Why is that . . . 'person' always poking his nose in our business?'

Joan frowns.

Ellie tries and fails to explain Ziggy Hook, so gives up and says he's a computer geek.

Joan shrugs.

'Haven't bothered with them since I finished working.'

Louisa nods her approval.

But then Ellie is serious.

'Ziggy wonders whether you know where your brother's phone might be?'

Joan frowns.

'Hum, no idea . . . like I've said, we hardly ever spoke or met each other.'

Fletcher and Louisa exchange glances.

'We'll have to ask the police I suppose,' he murmurs.

But now Louisa's frowning.

'They ought to have asked for permission to keep it.'

Fletcher shrugs and then feels guilty.

'Shall I call them?' he asks.

Louisa frowns again and looks at Joan.

'It might be better coming from you.'

Joan isn't keen but goes to find her own phone.

And five minutes later the mystery deepens.

'The police say they couldn't find it, although they've checked that he had one, but no-one's answering it . . . so either the attackers took it or . . .'

This makes for a longer silence, but then Ellie says she'll ask Ziggy, even though Louisa makes a face.

She goes to stand at the sea wall.

Not for long.

'As I expected he's already tried,' she murmurs, ' but he says it's not blocked, still working and he's monitoring it, trying to find if it's being used and in a bit he'll be able to give me a 'triangulation'.'

Joan is the only one astonished by this, but the others all shrug.

This is a bit of a conversation stopper, so she goes to make some more coffee.

'Do you think the attackers will have taken it?' asks Louisa, but even Ellie can only shrug at that.

'You would think they would, especially if they had communicated with him recently,' she offers.

But then Ellie's phone is burbling, so she goes again to the sea wall.

It's never a long conversation with Ziggy and Ellie comes back.

'He says it's almost certainly in his house. He's sure it's turned off, so most people won't know how to find it, so he wants me to go back and he'll use my phone to get a better signal.'

So Fletcher says he'll go with her.

The two of them and Rollo go back through the tunnel under the wall and then along to his house.

Ellie listens to what Ziggy's saying as he gets there.

He's already hooked through hers, so he tells her to stop opposite the doorway.

She stands there waiting.

'You've got a key, yeah,' asks Ziggy. She confirms.

'Ok, go in through the front door and go slowly.'

Fletcher follows her.

They get halfway down the corridor just before the doors to the front rooms, when he says stop.

'It's to your left, underneath the floor – probably under a floorboard.'

Fletcher follows her into the room and she asks him to pull up the carpet.

Not easily done as it's a heavy Persian one.

Even then it's not obvious, until Rollo goes sniffing and then barks at a particular spot.

Ellie kneels down and sees the hairline gap at either end of a foot long piece in the polished wood .

Wishing she didn't bite her nails so much; she finds her girl scout multiblade knife in her bag and eventually prises it up to reveal a couple of bags and . . . a small phone.

Ziggy says to get out quick in case there's some kind of warning device, which was sound advice as just as they were closing the front door there was a big explosion, which blew the windows out.

Fortunately there was no-one on this section of the wall, so the two of them were able to pretend they were just passing. A man turned up with a dog and said he'd call the fire brigade and then they slipped away back down to Joan's.

Ziggy must have heard the explosion and told Ellie not to try and turn the phone on or maybe that will blow up as well!

'Send it to me asap,' he says.

All this excitement means that Joan has to find another bottle of wine and another lot of coffees.

Ziggy tells Ellie to put the phone in a bin or something.

Joan produces an old safe box where she kept all her papers and gives it to her.

Then Fletcher and Ellie set off to Ziggy's, while Louisa stays with Joan, as she thinks the police will be wanting to know who was in the house.

*   *   *

URSULA

Janet and I weren't told about the imminent arrival of Ellie, so it was a bit of a surprise when she bursts through the door followed by her equally excitable dog.

We only get a couple of 'Hi's' and 'glad to see yous' before she goes into Ziggy's room, which is always a squeeze, but maybe not for someone as lithe as her.

So I go to put the kettle on and then remember Janet's bought us a coffee machine, which I'm still struggling to fathom, so she comes and does it . . .which makes me feel even more redundant.

Anyway Ellie and Ziggy aren't saying much, something to do with a phone which she's brought with her.

The two of them are either muttering words I know I wouldn't understand or silent.

But eventually I do here a collective sigh of relief and a little 'yow' from Ellie.

So now she comes back to us.

'Well, hello!' I say, feeling like an ancient aunt, which actually I think I am as far as Ellie's concerned.

She grins and gives me a hug and then Janet.

'So what skulduggery are you up to now?' she asks.

Ellie takes a big breath and tells us.

Well, at her speed I soon get lost, but understand that this phone belongs to an old guy who's been killed and it might give them some idea who the bad guys are?

'So who are the bad guys?' asks Janet coming straight to the point as usual.

'Ah,' says Ellie, her eyes going wider than ever, 'well, the phone belongs to a man who's an art dealer in Berwick, but he's been killed and so we're hoping Ziggy can get onto the phone and find who he's been dealing with, hopefully the people who stole some extremely valuable Elizabethan jewellery from a big house up in the hills beyond Jedburgh . . .' and she pauses for breath.

'Whoah,' says Janet.

I just shake my head.

Then Ziggy gives one of his whoops, so Ellie and Janet go to see what he's found out, while I find myself twiddling Rollo's ears, which is one thing I am good at.

In the event, I eventually take him outside and he enjoys a bit of stick chasing together in the garden, until he tires of that and sets off snuffling in the overgrown weeds, which I haven't got round to dealing with yet.

So it's a good hour before Janet and Ellie reappear looking a little bit less excited.

I go to make some more coffee but listen in to their conversation.

It appears that Ziggy has managed to 'access the phone' but is now trying to 'recover' some messages which are 'encrypted' – a word I had to look up but was none the wiser, other than it's some form of secret language like children use nowadays.

But now Ellie's going on about the historical significance of Berwick in Elizabethan times which seems to be her next big investigation, which begs the question about 'when she'll stop being the eternal student and get a proper job' as my mother might have *said – which hopefully doesn't mean I'm turning into her?!*

'God forgive me!' I say out loud . . . which gets a momentary frown from both of them but then they carry on.

*   *   *

Xavi has found a small flat just back from the walls near Henry's place, neither of them wanting to be with the sort of people who use the YHA, like old folk and families.

The flat is ridiculously expensive, but has all mod cons, so it suits both of them and they're not short of money and they can get Voudra to do any dangerous online investigations from her heavily guarded system.

But also in the event it allows them to keep a watch on Henry's house, which is just as well, because when the police have finished some other people investigate.

A young woman with a boisterous spaniel and an old guy, who might be her grandfather, who seem to have a key and then they leave looking rather excited.

Otka pursues them as they head off quickly and go down under the walls, so she follows and finds them sitting with a couple of older women.

She goes past until there's a gap in the houses but stands at the sea wall pretending to be taking pictures. Until the girl and the 'grandfather' set off walking urgently.

She watches them, calling Xavi to get the car.

Fortunately, their car is in the same carpark as theirs, so it's easy to follow them.

Half an hour later as they get to Kelso, Otka begins to get more worried, she's asked Voudra to check out the car and she quickly finds it belongs to a woman called Louisa Cunninghame, who lives in a large property east of Kelso, which means they're not going there.

'So that means the older woman who's stayed in Berwick is the owner and not either of this couple,' she murmurs to Xavi, who shrugs, chasing this car at this speed not easy to keep up, especially on an otherwise empty road.

In the end the car makes a right turn on the outskirts of Kelso and heads north and she hears Voudra's voice saying she's tracking the car now, so they can stay back.

So it's another fifteen minutes or so when they're round the back side of the Eildon Hills and do a right left on the main road and head off towards Peebles.

'So why are they're going there?' mutters Otka.

But then the car disappears.

They get to a roundabout, which way?

Voudra swears.

'They turned left two hundred metres back onto a really small road running parallel to the Peebles road.

Xavi does a savage three-point turn and goes back to find the little turning and drops down to the river and over the bridge.

This road is tiny, only big houses and fields either side and driving fast he soon catches up with them and then it's only ten minutes before they pull off in front of a small cottage.

Xavi pulls in.

They watch the two passengers get out and go inside.

'What can you find out?' demands Otka.

Voudra sighs.

'Give me a minute.'

Xavi is leaning over the wheel but then gets out to stretch his back.

Otka frowns, Voudra's generally very quick finding out about people and places.

'Nada,' she murmurs, but the signal is breaking up.

Otka can see the big antenna sprouting out of the roof, which isn't surprising given the steepness of the slopes on both sides . . . so why can't Voudra find it?

'And now her signal's gone?'

She leans out the window and beckons to Xavi to get back in the car and they drive on, catching just a glimpse of the little cottage as they pass.

What's going on? Who are these people? She wonders.

She points at another layby and Xavi pulls in.

Voudra's voice returns.

'Wow,' she says, 'that's serious military level protection, don't even think of trying to get in,' she adds. 'In fact I should go a lot further, there's a café on the right in two miles or so.'

Otka tells Xavi and they continue on.

She's getting quite worried and he's desperate for a coffee and a cake.

*   *   *

I come awake with a start, which is becoming a habit.

It's not quite dawn and in any case there's a thick mist on the river. I huddle down inside my cloak and wait as the river disrobes itself from the blanket of grey, which is always a piece of magick to me. Birds start to find their voices in the bushes and trees around me and was that a fox barking? Then I remember the fireworks and noise of the previous evening and listen.

No more of that, I think, the celebrations all finished and the folk probably sleeping off a lot of food and drink.

But eventually the mist lifts and the sun breaks through, so I clamber down to the riverside, drink my fill and then set off, hoping I can find a fisherman's cottage or even an inn.

I'm thinking wearing a monk's cloth might give me some chance of alms, but then if they be Protestants that won't be good.

But now the land ahead is very flat, no trees by the river as far as I can see, although there are no houses or people either.

If I remember aright, this means I'm getting near to where the Whittader joins the Tweed, which means I'm only three leagues to Berwick, so perhaps if I get down near the river there'll be reeds and small trees.

It's not easy and my boots get very waterlogged, but slowly I get nearer and then it rains.

CHAPTER NINE

Walker is standing by his car on the lane looking out across the valley at Tomasz and Magda's residence.

He's told Rossi he doesn't need him today and to get onto any admin he needs to do. After he'd said that he couldn't think of any, but shrugs; he has far more difficult concerns to worry about.

For instance the feeling that the American husband might be thinking of dealing with the robbers himself, which might be very violent and highly illegal. His wife had hinted at this and he's had experience of rich people doing that before. People who think they're above the law and feel they can do what they want . . . often using excessive violence to deal with it.

And he knows a man like him can organise this without even being here, so what can he do?

Then there's Tomasz, a one-man killing machine, who won't hesitate to protect his family and anyone else he feels are vulnerable.

And then there's the weird tech guy along this lane, who always seems to be poking his nose in whenever he likes.

So, given the nature of these three difficult characters, he decides having the latter two on his side rather than trying to take on the first one alone.

But then a jeep pulls up beside him and he sees it's Gill in the driving seat.

She grins at him and steps down.

He frowns at the jeep, which isn't an old banger, but something very new.

'Courtesy of my dad,' she explains, 'old bastard left me a grouse moor and a couple of trout fisheries as well as the dilapidated cottage.'

He's still frowning.

'So, I sold them and got this.'

He shakes his head but can't help grinning.

*   *   *

Fletcher and Becket are chatting away, while Ellie is perched on a stool beside Ziggy trying to keep track of what he's doing, although even she can't really keep up. His fingers are like lightning and he's at least six screens open, flashing from one to another at different parts of the screen. He's also fiddling with some other screens on minicomputers, which she doesn't understand at all, except he says they're blocking attacks.

Basically he's playing a huge, many layered and multifaceted game in which he is both chasing and being chased using different tags and names.

'Gotcha!' he yells as one of the mini-screens shows a cartoon 'BANG' image and then goes black.

He leans back and sighs.

'It'll take them hours to get that back online!!'

But then he buckles down again, muttering to himself.

Ellie risks a question.

'Is there any chance they can find out where you are?'

He glances at her phone which she's turned off as he asked and shakes his head.

'As long as no-one else has their phone on here, we're safe.'

Ellie nods thinking Fletcher and Becket are both 'anti-nerds' and often can't remember where they've left their phones, which are old anyway – 'prehistoric' said Ziggy, who's temporarily blocked them anyway without telling them and they still haven't realised.

So that only leaves Ursula, who is fairly unique in that she's never owned one!!

Speaking of her, she arrives with coffee and chocolate biscuits, which Ziggy attacks without a thankyou and Ellie decides to take hers and find the 'odd couple'.

Unusually, they're reminiscing, which is a rare event in itself - the terrible misdemeanours and illegal methods they used 'to catch the bad guys'.

But now she's getting restless and wanting to be doing something, she even pulls her phone out, but just in time remembers Ziggy's rules, which convinces her she needs to be elsewhere.

*   *   *

What she doesn't know is that the big house has visitors.

Tomasz has spent most of yesterday and since very early this morning, trying to make the house as secure as possible, which isn't easy when most of the incumbents are female, old and young. Obviously he hasn't said this, but the strongest thing about this house is the number of rooms and stairs; so that someone who doesn't know them, it's like a four-storey labyrinth. And then there are three secret tunnels and hideaways, which include exit routes, including the one that comes up in the gardener's cottage further downhill.

He and Magda grew up in them and spent hours chasing each other and their friends, meaning they can even find their way around without torches if needed . . . but he has garnered as many as he could find.

So seeing the sleek black Daimler glide into the courtyard isn't exactly a surprise.

Everyone except he and his mother retreat to the agreed hiding places.

He waits till the two equally sleek public-school boys get out the car and do their regulation suit checks and pretending to take in the view.

Then he nods to his mother who gives him a wink! She's not had such excitement since she was running from the Stasi back in the fifties.

She goes to the kitchen door and grabbing the walking stick which she certainly doesn't need, opens the door slowly and gingerly steps outside.

Whatever they've been told, these two stooges can't cope with a deaf and crippled Polish lady, who keeps asking them if they're the plumbers.

Tomasz gets a text from Magda up in the attic saying there's no-one coming up the back lane, so this must be the stalking party not the huntsmen.

He rushes out, shouting in Polish at his mother, telling her she mustn't talk to strangers and a lot of other nonsense.

They then have a little spat and she hobbles off back inside, where the limp disappears and the gun is retrieved from behind the door.

'Sorry about that,' he gushes, 'she's still fighting the war, I'm afraid.'

The slightly smaller 'chap' smiles and offers his hand, while Tomasz is telling himself that if he says he's called Fanshaw he mustn't shoot him.

'DI Holloway, sir,' showing him his badge, 'and this is DS Browning,' as the John Cleese gangler unfolds a hand from the end of his arm.

'What can I do for you?' he asks.

Holloway clears his throat, as if he's in a Noel Coward play.

'Er . . . well . . . sir, we know that Lady Catherine Hadley and her daughters are staying with you at the moment.'

Tomasz frowns.

'Hadley?'

He shakes his head.

'Don't know the lady? Have you got the right house?'

Holloway smiles.

'You may know her by her first married name, sir . . . Turnbull.'

Tomasz laughs.

'Oh, Cate, forgot she'd married 'an American B list'.'

Holloway manages another smile but Tomasz knows he's getting under his thin skin.

'Yes, sir, but are she and her daughters here?'

'What? Oh, staying with us, you mean? Well, they were but they left two days ago.'

Holloway has to look at his shoes, which are very shiny.

'I see, sir, but we were pretty certain she was still here.'

Tomasz shrugs and then laughs.

'Well, I'm not doolally yet young man . . . I'm pretty certain that they left yesterday morning, going to France, house in the Massif Central I think, for some hols.'

Holloway sighs and puts his hand in his pocket, which Tomasz prays his mother doesn't think he's reaching for a gun.

But it's only a card.

'Well, we'll just have to track them down . . . sir, but if you are in contact with them, please tell them to give me a call.'

It's at this moment that Fletcher and Ellie arrive in a flurry of gravel, Fletcher getting out and putting on his best menacing face.

Stooges exit stage left.

Inside, five minutes later everyone's laughing, although Helena pretends to be offended by Tomasz's rendering of her performance.

But now, Tomasz is on his phone.

When Magda asked who he was calling he just said 'cavalry' . . . which made her eyes go wide.

'Really?' she wondered, thinking who that might be, then thinking of the last party 'the cavalry' came here . . . 'raucous' and ' extreme' comes to mind – men his age who are no longer in the army but can't stop being . . .

He reappears.

'Is that necessary?' she asks.

He shrugs.

'Well . . . if nothing else . . .' but his phone is burbling.

He walks away, giving instructions to someone, who turns out to be just down the road.

Apparently, they are some of the cavalry and five minutes later a large, dirty landrover surges up at the stables in a wave of gravel.

A blond-haired giant jumps down, turns to pull out a crate of bottles and strides across to the terrace followed by his opposite, a small dark, weaselly guy, lugging two army bags.

There's a lot of fist pumping and ribald laughter, they're introduced as Will and Dex, but then Tomasz takes them off 'to talk tactics'.

*   *   *

Otka leaves Xavi tucking into the sort of food she thinks is for grandmothers and small children.

The small house they passed back along the lane was scary. Why has someone in the middle of nowhere have such excessive online defence . . . and is it a coincidence that it's only a mile or so away on the other side of the valley from the highly decorated soldier's family house?

She's always suspicious of coincidences like that.

She's told Voudra to investigate . . . carefully.

Nothing yet?

But then she's calling.

'Suspicious car just leaving the big house . . .'

'What do you mean suspicious?' asks Otka.

'Not police,' says Voudra, 'hire car from Edinburgh, now parked up in Galashiels . . . can't find them.'

'What do you mean 'not police'?!'

'I checked - no such names not even on the Home Office list.'

Otka's thinking.

'So next thing will be the armed 'gorillas'?'

'Maybe . . . probably . . .' says Voudra.

'Um . . .' is all Otka can say and cuts the call.

She goes to find Xavi.

'We need to get back to the big house . . . I think they're going to be attacked by the husband's thugs.'

Xavi is open mouthed, but then follows her to the car, cake in hand.

'What can we do?' he mutters, crumbs all over.

110

'Well, first off, we can warn them . . . but then . . . I think we need to go to the 'little house in the woods'.'

Xavi frowns again and then remembers.

So, he starts the car as she makes another call.

*   *   *

Actually Ziggy has started taking his kit apart already because he's agreed with Tomasz, that the people they're dealing with won't take kindly to being spied on and he needs to be somewhere safer.

And who should offer to provide that?

To Tomasz's surprise, Ziggy's already had another invitation which he has enthusiastically taken up.

From Louisa!

Her last husband had an underground bunker built at the height of the Cold War, when he thought there was serious chance the Russians might press the button. Although the bunker has thick concrete walls, there are pipes which allow for water and a generator, so even better than the little cottage.

'Absolutely' perfect was Ziggy's response and so that's where he's heading, having asked a young guy who he's been communicating with for some time to join him. Questions about sexual orientation not discussed, but . . .

And now he knows there are potential reinforcements arriving, so he alerts Becket, who sees the little car slowing down at their gate.

Otka gets out of the car to find she's a target.

A tall older woman, dark hair, dark eyes and a shotgun.

Otka puts her hands up.

The woman nods at Xavi.

'Him, too,' she growls.

But then Ziggy shouts: 'they're okay, I was expecting them.'

Becket frowns but doesn't put the gun down and insists on checking their clothing before urging them inside.

111

They are astounded by Ziggy's set up, even though he's taking it apart, but then Otka nods.

'So that's what's providing your security! Awesome!'

Ziggy shakes his head.

'Not so bad yourselves,' he winks.

Otka frowns, questions like 'when?' 'how?' 'how long for?' jumping about in her head.

'It's okay,' he says, 'I realised you were 'angels' some time ago . . . I especially liked the Paris job . . . couldn't have done better myself, especially not the flying bits . . . terrifying!'

Now Janet's staring at Ziggy and back at this tiny woman who she thinks she could crush with one hand.

'You mean you know these people?' she demands.

He shrugs as he puts another piece of his kit into a box.

'Well, not 'know' like I know you, but I've been following them for some time, exhilarating stuff!'

Becket knows Ziggy doesn't tell anyone everything . . . it would be impossible anyway – too much and too difficult to understand.

And now she can see that these two strangers are staring at him as well.

'Scaree . . .' whispers Otka, while Xavi's just shaking his head.

All through this Ellie is starting to find herself sidelined and not sure where she should be going, so she says she's going to Louisa's as well, but thinking about Henry's sister back in Berwick, considers she might be better investigating there.

Not sure which?

But knows her instinct is generally right.

She whispers this to Ziggy who nods his understanding, although there's a slight frown like he's thinking of something else . . . which generally means giving her a job.

'When you're there, buy a new phone and call me.'

She stares at him, but he just makes a face so she calls Rollo and sets off to her car.

It's only as she's reversing out that she sees Fletcher in her mirror.

Without a word spoken he gets in and she drives off . . . both of them feeling a bit treacherous, but not sure why.

*   *   *

URSULA

My head is spinning.

One minute I'm carrying a tray of coffees . . . to find Ziggy putting his things in boxes.

'Where are you . . . what . . ?' I ask, trying not to shake so much I'll spill all the drinks.

'WE are going to Louisa's - including you - so go pack a bag.'

I stand transfixed.

One, he's never spoken to me in such an abrupt fashion and then, two, I'm foolishly thinking what do you put in a bag to go to Louisa's?

I know how to do as I'm told but . . .

And when I come back from my room with 'the bag' not really knowing what I put in it, there's two new people standing in the kitchen.

A small woman, no bigger than a twelve-year-old and a slightly taller man whose really muscly legs come down from a very tight pair of cycling shorts.

Becket's got a heavier gun than usual clenched in her hands and sort of keeping guard.

I catch the last few words which seem to mean they're going to go with us to Louisa's as well.

What's going on?

Now everyone's taking Ziggy's boxes out to cars and then minutes later we're a three-car motorcade rumbling along the lane heading for Louisa's.

I don't even have time to say goodbye to my 'shadowy friends' and start worrying about them although I know that's . . .
I try not to cry . . .

And fail.

*   *   *   **

RALPH?

Someone's calling me.
Ralph?
Is that my mother?
I'm wet.
Where am I?

Then I remember.

I'd reached the Whittader and saw a boat, but then someone was there and I had to hide in the reeds.
I couldn't see him, but decided to wait until he went away.
I'd peeped over the reeds to see that he was using the boat to go out into the Whittader just up from where it was eaten by the Tweed.
He didn't go until it was dusk, but he did leave the boat on this side and I watched him slowly walking back through the fields, but then I saw the fireflies in the distance and found the abandoned upturned boat and prayed no-one found me.

CHAPTER TEN

Magda makes up her mind.

She can't let Tomasz and his cavalry try to stop what she thinks will be a blood bath.

She's talked to Catherine, who is very frightened and thinks her husband is so angry that he will send reinforcements who won't take no for an answer.

So she goes outside and calls Walker.

'Who were these two officers?' he asks, thinking the worst and hearing their names confirms it. Not likely up here in Scotland. Not that the 'men in black' would bother to communicate with him and the silence from Edinburgh speaks volumes. Not their case, not looking or listening.

'I'll see what I can do, but don't hold your breath,' he says, then feels that's pathetic, so he adds 'I'm on to it.'

Gill listens and looks away.

'So, it's just you and me?'

'Have you still got a gun?' he asks.

She grins.

'Better than that, I've got my father's armoury in the back.'

He frowns.

'I was hoping we might get back-up.'

'Yeh, right,' she snarls.

They're both staring across at the big house.

'If I was back in Manchester I could have an army in half an hour . . .'

'Um . . . pity, and Rossi comes from the wrong end of Italy, doubt he even knows any Mafiosi,' muses Gill.

He shrugs.

'An army?' she whispers. 'How long would it take the gas board to send someone if we reported a leak?' she murmurs as she types it in.

'Less than an hour, ' she confirms.

Walker stares at her . . . but can't help grinning.

'And the fire brigade!'
But then they think about it.
'No use doing it now.'

'What we need is the attackers' contact details?' he murmurs.
Gill frowns.
'Going to be off grid.'
'So, who do we know who could find them?'
Gill starts the engine.
'He's just along the lane here.'

But they're too late.
Gill has a number.
Ziggy answers.
She explains.
He tells her what he's doing and he'll be up and running in an hour.

Walker frowns at her.
'You won't believe this,' she whispers.
She tells him.
His eyes like saucers.

*   *   *

Ellie's persuaded Fletcher to go back to Berwick again.
To be honest, he's relieved. Even when he was a younger more gung-ho sort of chap, he'd never carried a gun, saying that having one only makes other people get them, which he doesn't hesitate to back up with 'deaths caused by shooting' records showing a consistent increase since when he was in the job.
So she drives and he asks the questions.
'This Henry chap seemed very secretive?'
She nods.
'Yeh, but I'm more interested in the people who stole the stuff from the American's house.'

116

'You mean that skinny young woman and the dwarf?'

She makes a face.

'Ziggy has sent me a few videos of their shows, they're amazing acrobats and trapeze artists, which is obviously very useful if you're breaking into second floor rooms in heavily protected properties.'

He frowns.

'Like Magda's friend's house.'

'Exactement,' she whispers.

He glances over to see moving images on her screen.

'Wow!' he gasps, seeing the skinny young woman flying through the air to be caught by the 'dwarf'.

'So where are they now?,' he asks thinking they'd be good reinforcements for Tomasz's 'army.

'Don't know,' says Ellie, 'maybe . . .' but he knows her mind's elsewhere.

And now she's looking out the window.

'They'll all be okay, but I still need to figure out where Henry Grey might hide things.'

Fletcher sighs.

'Well, a big old house like he lived in must have hundreds of places to hide things . . . like his phone.'

Ellie sighs.

'No . . . I've a feeling he didn't do that with things . . . that might get him into trouble.'

Fletcher frowns.

'Why?'

'Did you look at the paintings in his rooms?'

Fletcher frowns again, knowing he can't tell a Van Gogh from a Constable.

Inevitably she had managed to snap a few of them in the room where the phone was found.

'I don't know what he's got in other rooms but most of these are Italian masters, a Titian and a Michaelangelo . . . which can't be the real things, they'd be worth millions . . . even good copies would be thousands.'

Fletcher shrugs.

'So . . .'

She sighs.

'I don't know, but I bet he's got lots of things hidden away . . . somewhere else?'

Fletcher shakes his head.

'Where do we start?'

Half an hour later they're parked up near what Fletcher thinks he might have start calling it 'Ellie's church'.

She sits staring at it, then fingers her mobile.

Then she sighs.

'The thing is this church wasn't built until a hundred years after the walls – unbelievably on the orders of Mr Cromwell.'

Fletcher frowns.

'You mean Oliver? Wasn't he a protestant?'

She sighs again.

'Exactement.'

'But it says it's a Church of Scotland?' he murmurs, thinking he's drowning not swimming already . . . having never got past the Norman Conquest at school.

'Uhuh . . . that's later . . .' she mumbles.

She gets out and sets off to the gates, preceded by a jaunty Rollo, so he follows on.

This time she goes 'widdershins' – a word she loves, telling Rollo to behave.

Fletcher stops at a gravestone, the writing's in Latin, but the name says Nisbet . . . sounds like a biscuit.

But then he looks up and she's disappeared.

Finds her round the corner reading her phone.

For once she can't get Ziggy, although she knows he won't take long to get online at Louisa's, so she tries someone else.

The town archivist? But the library's shut for today and tomorrow, no reason given?

She frowns, who else might know?

She's tried some of the numbers for the historical society, but they're either not answering or no longer available?

What's going on?

Maybe they've all been killed? 'To silence them?'

'Silence who?' says a voice.

She turns quickly.

A large woman, no, a 'lady', she recognises the type, often the vicar's wife or someone who regards themselves as 'important' in a sort of self-appointed role in church business.

Ellie laughs.

'Ah, you caught me out, talking to myself again,' she laughs.

The 'lady' frowns.

'You're a bit too young to be doing that, young lady, and is this dog yours?'

Ellie looks round guiltily thinking he's peed on a grave or even worse, but no, he's accepting a biscuit from the lady.

'Lost mine a few months ago, decided to do without for now, too upsetting when they die.'

Ellie stares at her.

'I'm so sorry, I can't begin to even think about that.'

'Um,' says the woman and looks at the gravestone she's standing next to.

'Actually I was looking for signs of the earlier medieval church.'

The woman frowns again.

'Don't know, but I know a man who will.'

'Who's that?'

'Henry.'

Ellie stares at the woman.

'Henry Grey?'

She cocks her head.

Ellie doesn't know what to say.

'But . . .'

'What?' demands the woman.

'I'm sorry . . . but he's dead . . . murdered . . .'

The woman nearly laughs, but then sees Ellie's face.

119

'No . . . but when? Why?'

Ellie can't believe she's got into this mess, so shakes her head.

'I don't really know, it's a friend of mine who, who was, his friend . . . Louisa Cunninghame.'

The woman's eyes grow even bigger.

'Louisa?'

Ellie frowns.

'You know her?'

The woman nods.

'Went to school together.'

Ellie doesn't know what to say and the woman is still shaking her head.

'Murdered, you say?'

Ellie nods, thinking she's in enough trouble already.

Then the woman frowns again.

'So how do you know Louisa?' sounding like 'how could she possibly know her?'

Ellie looks away, thinking how on earth she can explain her connection to Louisa and that's when Fletcher appears and how do you explain his relationship to Louisa?

But then the woman is telling her to come into the church and have a coffee . . . which turns into an interrogation, a long phone call with Louisa and then her and Fletcher commanded to have dinner at her house, which, of course, is on the Wall . . . and unbelievably, she's called Sybil Weatherstone!

Sybil?!

Ellie can't believe it.

*   *   *

Gill and Walker arrive at Tomasz and Magda's house.

Magda is waiting on the terrace.

Hengist has still enough energy to confront strangers, even if he's rather lame and his bark is fading and although Imelda's dog, Cushie, has appeared, she's not the barking kind.

120

They climb up the steps just at the same time as Tomasz comes out of the front door, and then gives his sister a hard stare.

'Did you ask them to come?' he demands, his one eye blazing.

She nods.

Walker waits for the reaction. Like watching a volcano having a change of heart.

They all wait as Tomasz calms down.

'I don't think you've realised what this man might do, even though he's the other side of the world,' he rasps.

Walker shrugs.

'You're right, I don't, but . . .'

'But 'nothing'?' Tomasz smirks.

Walker frowns.

'You're probably right . . .' he murmurs, thinking of the indifference of his superiors.

Tomasz shakes his head.

'Nearest armed unit to here? Edinburgh? Half an hour if they come in copters? Our bodies could be cold by then.'

Walker stares at him . . . thinking he's right again.

He shrugs.

'So, how's about we meet halfway . . . I'll make the call and we'll stay and lend a hand?'

Tomasz stares at him and then looks at Magda, who makes a face. Not what she's expecting, but then she recalls one or two whispers about this black cop from Manchester.

'Well,' says Tomasz, 'can't really say no to that . . .'

'Have you had any training?' says a gruff voice, a big guy standing at the end of the terrace, a machine gun dangling loosely over his shoulder.

Another guy appears on the left, his gun pointing to the sky.

Walker smiles and then he nods at Gill.

'And she's a one-woman army, martial arts expert . . .'

Gill doesn't smile.

'And I've got a jeep full of my dad's guns.'

So 'Magnificent Seven - Scene One' over, Magda shakes her head thinking there's only five of them, because she's not counting herself as she's always refused to have anything to do with guns . . . but then there's her mother, toting a gun at the kitchen doorway . . .

And then she wonders where Imelda is and sure enough she's leaning at her bedroom window. No gun, but scary enough anyway.

Walker still tries to get some backup, but after a short call, shrugs and shakes his head . . . and then Tomasz shakes his head at him, which tells him phones are all off here.

The next hour or so, Tomasz gives way to Will, who's more used to running a platoon.

First job is checking all the guns and ammunition and then positions, while Magda gets Catherine and the girls preparing a dinner for a dozen people, which is when she realises she's not missing Amelia and her kids. She knows the sudden holiday trip to Portugal, in term time, is just a cover for some assignation, which she isn't surprised about and can't remember the last time they had sex.

Gill's father's gun collection includes lots of ammunition as well, although Helena is the one who's got the most experience with them, Tomasz having given up such heavy weapons a long time ago, and she has also unearthed his father's collection.

Then Tomasz takes over to give people positions, although he and Will think they won't be coming up the hill to the terrace unless they're either mad or stupid.

They've thought about an aerial approach, men dropping from copters onto the roof, but then they reject that as well as being too dangerous, even in the dark, especially when Tomasz shows them the big lamps which were put up for his father's seventieth birthday celebrations and never taken down.

The weak point is the driveway from the back road, although the approach is a long winding lane through huge fields to the top of the hill, someone coming either way would be seen from miles away.

By eleven o'clock everyone's wanting to go to bed and Will thinks it would be difficult to mount an attack in the dark not knowing the building or who's where in it.

So the 'squad' is split into pairs including Catherine and Mary insisting on taking their turn.

And now the house is in darkness. Only torches allowed if needed.

Walker lies on a bed. Eyes open.

Gill is on first watch.

Even if they pull this off, he knows it will be the end for him and her as police officers, which he doesn't think will bother her, but he's been a police officer since he was eighteen. What would he do?

*   *   *

Louisa gets back home to find she's been invaded.

She's okay with that, especially as she's getting to think the huge pile is far too much for her and Fletcher and then realises he's become permanent, when did that happen?

She also realises the little car parked rather randomly means that Ziggy's co-opted the circus clowns as well.

Ziggy didn't need any help finding the key to the bunker and when she shouts down the steps its only Becket who replies.

But then she sees Ursula looking lost at the kitchen window.

She goes back inside to her and without thinking and very much out of character, she puts her arms round her. Neither of them would regard themselves as 'touchy feely' people, but after tightening up Ursula relaxes.

'I can't remember if you've ever been here before? asks Louisa.

Ursula shakes her head, deciding not to tell her that she's seen inside her house on Ziggy's screen and it's even more overwhelming in the reality.

So five minutes later Louisa's on her first G&T and has persuaded Ursula to have a T&G.

And then the house phone rings.

*   *   *

URSULA

I always feel awkward when someone I'm with gets a phone call. If I stay where I am I feel as though I'm hovering and earwigging, which I'm definitely not.

But here at Louisa's in this huge room and her voice filling it with 'darlings' and 'no, reallys!', I have to go away . . . out of the room and find myself in the library, but quickly realise that it's been taken over by Ellie, the scattering of books and papers all over the table, the seats and the floor the giveaway.

I know it looks like chaos, but I also know from experience that this is her way of working and she would know if any one of these apparently random placings was fingered or moved.

I go to stand at the window.

The garden grumbling to itself as the winter stretches into spring and everything's on hold until it gets warmer. But even so it's astonishing. Huge trees and bushes hiding the house from anyone daring to look.

I open the French window and go out.

The daffodils are well on here, doubtlessly urged on by Louisa's gardeners, who must be a longsuffering gang, always having to be on top of everything.

I keep going until I reach the riverbank and stand looking at the water surging along, weeks and weeks of rain engorging it into a torrent . . . but then realise I'm homesick . . .

Which makes me laugh at myself . . . home?

And then something astonishing happens.

First, there's a kingfisher darting about . . . not actually rare here, but . . . a black raven standing on a rock in the middle of the torrent, it's eye flickering in the light.

Then over to my left there's my hare . . . cleaning its ear and . . . finally the slightest outline of a thin dog . . .
they've followed me here!

*   *   *

Otka and Xavi are sitting in the car.

Xavi's holding his breath, not knowing what Otka's thinking, but knowing that he'll get nothing if he asks, when she's looking like this – what she calls 'how to get out of this hole she's dug'.

Looking out the window, he thinks it's not such a bad hole to be in, Louisa's house and gardens the sort of place they'd might think of checking out.

Given the sighs and the shaking head he thinks Otka's already doing the search.

Otka sighs and closes her phone.

She gets out of the car and he follows.

Knocking at the door proves fruitless, so Otka takes hold of the ornate handle and pushes.

No alarms, no dogs, no servant coming to see who they are, so they venture further in.

A huge entrance hall with four doors off, whilst facing them a staircase which ascends to a huge painting where it bifurcates into two smaller stairs right and left.

Otka stares at the painting; if that's a real Watteau!? It can't be? She resists the urge to take pictures of it.

Looking upwards there's a round window like a Roman oculus which must be two or three storeys above them.

Obviously neither of them has any fear of heights, but still it's dizzying to look up.

Otka shakes her head.

'What a show we could put on here,' she whispers, her eyes sparkling.

Xavi can only nod and can't help checking out the flying distances.

As there is no welcoming servant, they set off to the left where they can hear someone talking, to find themselves in another huge space with lots of windows and at the far end, Louisa standing talking on a phone.

She beckons them on, so they do as they're told and sit on the chairs she indicates, although then Otka can't resist going to one of the windows and looking out into the garden.

Louisa continues her call, laughing and then agreeing to set off as soon as she can and then ends the call.

She doesn't immediately turn to them, just holds the phone to her chest . . . but then sparks back into life and smiles.

'Well,' she says, 'I'm afraid you've been responsible for a lot of . . . connections . . . which I'm sure you didn't intend but this latest one is . . . intriguing.'

Otka and Xavi can only look puzzled.

Louisa shakes her head.

'I know you didn't mean to harm Henry and I'm certain you didn't kill him, but I'm afraid you may have caused it . . .'

They both frown and glance at each other, Xavi shrugs.

'Anyway, I'll tell you in the car . . . you can leave yours here.'

This doesn't sound like a suggestion, so they comply.

Two hours later they're all sitting around a huge, polished table, definitely not IKEA, in an enormous room which has a splendid view across the Tweed estuary.

At the top of table sits Sybil trying to remember when she last had such diverse and interesting dinner party guests.

Opposite her is Louisa, looking as regal as always. To her left the strange ex-detective who seems to have inexplicably become her longtime 'partner', the word 'lover' seems inappropriate, especially with his different coloured eyes.

Then this slight young thing called Eleanora, whose green eyes shine like lasers as her attention fizzes from one person to another, like she's recording them.

And then the two circus performers. Both small, Otka, the girl like a fairy and Xavi, a mini wrestler.

Fortunately, Baxter was able to supply a decent cut of beef, although it turns out that the fairy and Ellie are vegetarians so extra forage needed to be found.

Lots of conversation and stories from the acrobats, but eventually the serious questions can't be avoided, so, yes, they did steal the necklace and the glasses from the big house.

'But . . .' whispers Otka, 'we were asked to take them, even though normally we wouldn't touch anything as historically 'important' as those objects.'

Sybil and Louisa frown at each other.

'You mean you were approached and they were specified?'

Otka blinks.

Sybil's eyes go wide.

But Otka holds up a finger, which is not elegant, in fact crooked.

'We did take other things, much less precious, but less dangerous to pass on,' she whispers.

'So who asked you to do this?'

Otka shakes her head.

'No idea . . . that's how it works.'

Louisa and Sybil exchange frowns again.

Otka sighs.

They wait.

'We get a call. No names. Phone deleted after the call . . . the articles they want, where they are, security details if they have them and the deal.'

Now the two ladies are speechless – an event most of the people who know them would say 'you're lying'.

'But . . .' asks Ellie, softly, 'how did Henry get involved?'

'Ah . . .' says Otka and she frowns and looks away, which Fletcher suspects means she's going to tell a lie.

'Well . . . he's one of our contacts, I mean a buyer for other people . . . he did the bargaining . . . no names . . . but . . .'

Again she looks away. Fletcher gives Ellie a look.

'He got back to us, asking if we were sure of the provenance . . . their 'authenticity',' blushing with the difficulty of pronouncing the word.

'Because he knew how valuable they were presumably,' murmurs Sybil.

Otka nods.

'Which is why we sent them to him . . . because WE didn't know how . . . ' for once she's stuck for the English words and mutters to Xavi who shrugs, so she chooses French.

'Sans prix . . .'

RALPH?

Dawn.

Thick mist.

I'm wet.

The man is nowhere to be seen so I swish through the sedge to find the boat . . . to find another man waiting.

Standing like a post. In fact, leaning on an oar.

He's dressed in a long grey coat.

I stand watching, not sure what to do.

'Dost thee want to cross t'other said,' he asks, in a hoarse voice, which seems to echo over the surging water.

I couldn't speak.

He didn't seem to move but now I can see his face. Long and gaunt, thin grey hair, his hood hiding the dark sockets of his eyes.

I manage to nod and find my voice, although it sounded like his.

'I've nae monaie.'
A hushed breath shifts the reeds.
'Nae bother,' whispers the reply.

And then I'm huddled in the prow of the boat, while he pushes it out into the river and then sits and begins to row . . . slow at first, but then as we get out into the current he starts pulling harder on the downstream side to stop us from going out into the Tweed, which looks heavy and ominous.

Just when I think we'll end up getting caught by the bigger river, he's reached the shallower water and a few moments after we're beached on the bank.

I get out and cross myself, then turn to thank my rescuer to find him going back across the river without another word spoken.

In a few moments he's disappeared in the mist, just the sound of the river and the lonely call of a bird.

But in the hush that follows I can hear something else.

Something rushing in the air.

I watch as the sun rises and then I see it - a bridge like the one back upstream but much longer.

I can't see if there are any monsters, but I know I need to get beyond it, if I'm going to get to Berwick, so I set off, even though I'm shaking with fear.

CHAPTER ELEVEN

Tomasz can hear a dog barking and comes awake with a start.

Turns to look for Imelda and finds her side is cold.

He leaps out of the bed and realises he's still dressed and a glance through the window knows it's just dawn.

Not quite sure who's supposed to be on lookout now but certain it's not him, he sets off down the stairs.

To find his mother in the kitchen stirring a big pot of porridge and Imelda at the doorway, gun leaning against the jamb.

They both stare at him and then smile . . . who wouldn't at a man with only one shoe on and his hair looking like he's put his fingers in an electric socket.

He realises this as he glances at the mirror on the wall and can't help laughing and feeling sheepish, but then tries to be serious . . . the man in charge . . . which makes the other two smile again.

'Okay,' he says, 'never been a morning person . . .', which both of them know is not true, so he gives in and sits down.

Imelda turns to look out at the valley.

Helena stirs the porridge.

Gradually the rest of the 'platoon' arrive.

Catherine insists taking on the porridge stirring and Mary lays tables in the breakfast room, which hasn't seen so many folk for ages . . . having been Helena's little workplace with her sewing machine now pushed onto a side table.

The last to arrive are Will and Dex who'd been on guard in the small hours, looking the worst for wear but that might have been the vodka they were using to keep awake.

Although there's some effort to be normal there's a tension always in the background, half of them having a lot of experience of warfare and the other half none.

By seven thirty Walker thinks that's an okay time to ring his superiors and leaves the room, without saying what he's doing, although the 'soldiers' give each other looks and Dex silently follows him.

Walker isn't confident of getting any help at all, in fact he's expecting a serious bollocking, but then is surprised to find himself listening to a very senior officer, who he's never even heard of before.

He doesn't get to say very much, except a lot of 'yes' and 'no sirs', but the gist of what this man is saying is that they're aware of the husband's attitudes and potential for ordering violent actions according to US contacts . . . although until he shows his hand there's little they can do . . . BUT they are onto him.

The conversation over, he stares out at the valley, which still has a morning mist down by the river and the main road.

But he's then aware of a quiet approach and turns to find Tomasz staring at him.

'So . . .' he murmurs, his eye patch glinting in the sun.

Walker shrugs.

'Better than I was expecting to be honest . . . I think they're feeling a bit . . . 'insulted'?'

Tomasz frowns.

Walker makes a face.

'Apparently some 'Lord or other' has been onto them talking about 'an embarrassing situation' and 'national security'.

Tomasz can't help but smile.

'Lord?'

Walker shrugs.

'Wouldn't say, but 'people in high places la-la, ' is what he's implying.

Tomasz looks away and shrugs.

'If my father was alive I dare say he'd know who that might be . . . but I've never had any truck with them.'

Walker frowns.

'But you are one of 'them' aren't you . . . Fettes, Scots Dragoon Guards, Afghanistan, highly decorated . . . etcetera?'

Tomasz's stare is icy, but then he looks away. Not public knowledge, meaning this guy has done some serious research.

Walker waits, knowing this is a crucial moment.

It's only less than a half a minute but it feels a lot longer.

'It's because I know what they're like that I'm not one of 'them' . . .'

The air is still, as if it is holding its breath.

Then Tomasz does something so unexpected, that Walker flinches and has to look away. He reaches up and flips his eye patch up, to reveal the full horror of the dark red hole that was once his eye.

'Did 'they' send anyone to look for me?.'

Walker forces himself to look back and is relieved that he's replaced the patch, although he knows he'll have nightmares for ever more.

'I was looked after by an Afghani woman, who found an old surgeon who managed to do the job, but he doubted I would survive, because he didn't have any antibiotics . . .'

Walker waits again.

Tomasz turns away.

'She found some, don't know how or where . . . I was out of it, unconscious, and screaming when I wasn't.'

Walker looks back at him.

A tear sliding down his face from the good eye.

Walker shudders and looks away again.

They stand there in silence . . . no . . . there are birds twittering and sheep bleating, which sound indecent somehow.

Afterwards Walker never told anyone about this . . . somehow or other it was so private it would have been a betrayal to repeat it to anyone else.

It can only have been a few moments but then he manages to put out his hand and put it on Tomasz's shoulder . . . and kept it there until the shuddering stopped.

No more words said.

Eventually, they turn and walk back up to the terrace.

To find the youngest daughter being comforted by her mother, the rest of the gang not meeting his eyes, apart from Will who shakes his head.

Catherine stares at Tomasz.

'She just forgot, okay, she's really sorry.'

It's only then that he sees the phone.

A rather vivid pink.

He can add two and two as quick as anyone but realises being angry won't help.

So he goes over to the girl and smiles.

'Hey, no worries, easily done, I do it all the time.'

He smiles at Catherine, who can't stop the tears.

Cups of coffee all round and then he asks to talk to her.

Takes her through into his father's room, although not much left of his presence anymore, all the diaries and records disappeared . . . he's no idea where to.

'Did he contact you?' he asks softly.

Anne nods and starts to weep again.

He waits.

'What did he say?'

She blows her nose and shrugs her shoulders.

'He wanted to know where we were and who was with us.'

Tomasz tries not to tense up and fails.

'But I didn't tell him . . . about you and your friends . . .'

He waits again, telling himself not to push, give her time.

'So, where does he think you are?'

She hesitates, is she going to lie? But she looks him in the eyes.

'I said we were in a hotel in Jedburgh . . .'

Tomasz frowns.

'Which one?'

'I said I didn't know and started crying . . . and then I realised he'd cut the call.'

Tomasz reaches out and puts his hand gently on her shoulder, realising he's absolutely no experience with children, so he's relieved when Catherine appears and takes her in her arms.

He mouths 'sorry' and she shakes her head.

Thinking that's also a signal to leave, he escapes.

Outside he reappraised the situation knowing Will is staring at him.

He goes over and they stand looking out over the valley.

'Well?' asks Will.

Tomasz shakes his head.

'If what's she's told me is true, I think he's none the wiser, but . . . it won't stop him coming for us, maybe with a bigger army.

*　　*　　*

Sybil insisted that everyone would stay overnight, saying it had been a long time since she'd had a full house.

No-one commented that even though there were six of them, there were still a couple of bedrooms to spare . . . and Otka waited until everyone was in their rooms, before slipping into bed with Xavi . . . and Fletcher was similarly commanded to come to Louisa's as well.

Ellie found herself in a room with a huge window looking out over the estuary and was so fascinated by the changes of light that she ended waking up just after midnight, on the window ledge, which had a thick cushion on it.

Just before she dozed off again, she thought she saw a figure out on the mud, but when she looked again it had gone. Although it then reappeared in a dream, slightly nightmarishly waking her up to find the moon shining on the mudflats. No figures, but still quite eerie.

As usual she was still the first to wake and after going to the loo - ensuite, of course - she went back to the window again to watch the sun come out of the sea, casting weird shadows across the oncoming tide.

Breakfast was in the 'breakfast' room! Of course!

Everyone else seemed to have had a good night's sleep, but Ellie couldn't help telling them about the figure walking the estuary.

Sybil frowns.

'I don't think so,' she insists, after Ellie had pointed to where she saw him.

'It changes all the time but the river's too strong for someone to cross . . . it's lethal,' she says.

Ellie doesn't argue, thinking she maybe dreamt it or mistook it for something else.

'But then there are a lot of ghosts here,' says Sybil.

Ellie stares at her.

'You should know, 'professor'!' says Louisa, winking at Ellie.

Ellie's feeling a bit got at, so she changes the subject.

'How on earth did you get to live here,' she asks, smiling at Sybil, whose eyes flash, briefly, before she laughs.

'Simple . . . I married the man who owned it and then he went and died.'

Ellie is mortified, but then Sybil laughs.

'It's twelve years ago, he's long gone and not coming back as a ghost as far as I know.'

Ellie nods.

'Okay, but you said there are lots of ghosts here?'

'Indeed . . . after all there's been a lot of people killed here, particularly before the Union.'

It's at this moment the two speakers realise they've got a rapt audience.

So both of them laugh and Sybil insists they leave the breakfast pots and 'walk the walls'.

It turns out that she has been a part-time walk guide, so they get a lively version, full of terrible stories.

They set off clockwise, because Sybil thinks it's unlucky to go the other way, which Ellie can't help telling her that in Yorkshire it's called widdershins.

So soon they're passing the oldest bridge 'built 1611-24' says Sybil looking over her glasses at Ellie.

'Not your period I'm afraid, although there were numerous earlier wooden ones, which were often washed away and this summer we're having the four hundred years celebrations.'

But Ellie's a bit worried about Rollo wanting to jump down onto the riverbank, which is very stony and a good eight feet below, so she gets pulled all the way to the old castle, where it's lower.

It's then that Ellie sees someone in the distance and realises the path goes all the way round the bend in the river.

Again she sees a figure, 'scuttling along' as though he's got a bad leg. She turns to see if the others can see him, but they've already turned up hill and looking at the White Walls, which is being explained by Sybil . . . and when she looks back he's disappeared.

Rollo is eager to catch up and they're soon up at the station.

Having crossed the road bridge, Ellie's on high alert again because there's plenty of signs saying steep drop, so she's

135

relieved when Sybil insists on taking them down to the church where they met the other day, saying she has a couple of jobs to do . . . and then tells Ellie she could take Rollo for a run on the edge of the golf course and find her way back to her house.

So it's only later when they've had lunch that Ellie says she'll go back to see the church again . . . which makes Fletcher smile, but then he senses she wants to go alone so doesn't offer to accompany her, even though that means he'll have to listen to Louisa and Sybil gossiping about a long list of mutual friends, well, the ones that are still alive.

Otka and Xavi have also disappeared so he goes to sit at the window and watch the river go by . . . meaning having a nap.

The weather has changed and a northeasterly wind is blowing, meaning the walk back is cold and windy, but the graveyard is below the walls and less blustery.

She passes the big house Louisa told them Lowry wanted to buy, but decided not to because it needed a lot of work.

As she glances up at it, she sees a figure slip behind one of the gate posts, as if they were playing hide and seek.

She looks back and yet again a head ducks away.

She frowns and shake her head.

Wonders if Ursula has seen them?

Back at the graveyard, she goes to find the gravestone.

'Cornelius Nisbet died 1795.'

Looking elsewhere, she knows that he must have been one of the first.

So why does this name mean something to her?

She looks round for Rollo . . . or rather anyone like Sybil and sees someone disappear round the corner.

She calls him.

It's only a few seconds before he appears, but long enough for her heart to start throbbing and now he's barking at her, which means he wants to show her something and he runs off again.

Heart in her mouth, her brain telling her it's probably a rabbit, she runs to the corner and there he is . . . snuffling around next to a gravestone . . . which is worrying, he's never done that before.

She calls him back and he hesitates.

So she calls him more forcefully and runs to see what he's found.

At first she doesn't see anything, but then it glints.

She bends down.

It's a coin.

An old coin.

A woman's face.

And then she sees the hand on the rim . . . which means!!!

Elizabeth the First 1556.

She realises she's stopped breathing and gulps air in, Rollo snuffles her and she nearly drops it.

Then she looks round.

No-one there?

She can't see anyone . . . but she feels watched.

She shivers.

Rollo licks her leg.

And now she sees it's next to another gravestone, sunken into the turf and the name is hardly visible it's so worn . . . but it's still legible.

Nisbet

She shivers again.

Gets to her feet trying not to drop the coin, because her hand is shaking.

She looks round.

No-one there.

She is feeling very unstable, a peculiar blend of ecstasy and terror but carefully wraps the coin in her hankie . . . stuffs it in her pocket and backs away from the gravestone.

Then whispering to Rollo she gets him to follow her to the gate and with one last frightened look she turns and runs.

*   *   *

URSULA

If you'd asked me how I'd feel if I was told we had to leave the little cottage and my 'guardians' behind I would have probably cried, but we're all here!

I've been out this afternoon and there they were, if anything a bit more cheerful than usual?

Anyway Ziggy seems happy too, saying the coverage is much better here, which means a lot more defences to put in, but then he's always happier if there's a problem; saying solving them is the best way to learn anything.

I was a bit more worried about Janet, but Louisa has a much better TV and a better signal and a lot of programmes she didn't even know existed, although Ziggy said she could have had them if she'd asked.

So now I'm thinking about what I might cook in Louisa's amazing kitchen. She'd rung last night to tell us they weren't coming back until this afternoon and she might be bringing a friend, although she can't be sure about Ellie because she's acting strange – seeing ghosts all over the place apparently – which doesn't surprise me – but nevertheless a bit worrying.

But then the phone rings and rings until I remember where it is and answer it.

It's Louisa saying they're staying on for another night because Ellie's found something really strange and insists she has to stay, even though she's scared but not able to explain what about.

I'm a bit relieved actually having had a rustle about in her kitchen and still not found a frying pan, so I go to tell Ziggy the news, which of course he already knows and points at one of the screens which is showing a large image of an old coin.

'Elizabeth the First' he tells me, 'with a hand'.

I can see it on the screen and yes there's a dismembered hand above a portrait of Elizabeth the First I assume.

'In good condition it could be worth thousands,' he says, as various sites showing lots of coins flicker away.

But then he mutters.

'But why it's in a graveyard, which only dates from the late eighteenth century, is a bit of a mystery.'

That is a bit puzzling . . . as if I know anything about coins.

But then his hands are whizzing all over the place, which tells me it's probably some kind of cyber-attack, so I go to the kitchen and think what we're going to eat which inevitably means Janet appears.

I tell her what's happening and she sighs.

'When will that girl stop digging things up?'

I can only shrug . . . after all she is a historian . . . and that's what they do . . . although she did tell me Elizabeth the First was not her period . . . so maybe that's changed.

And at least I do know a bit about her, but I'm not going to tell her that!

RALPH

Yesterday was terrifying.

After the strange bridge of rushing creatures, the river side was very flat and then there were trees up the hillside even though there was a path along by the mudflats. I recognised the salmon fishing pools, so I knew I must be getting to the White Castle walls, which will be still manned.

But then I saw another bridge.

High, high above the castle like it was built by a giant spider, all the black threads holding it up.

And then the spider came, rattling along the top.

Luckily it was just when there was willow trees near the river and I was able to hide.

And just as dusk was falling I saw the lights of the town coming on . . . more and more until I thought it must be burning, but there's no scent of smoke, so I continue . . . the thought of a kitchen with an open fire, a pig roasting on the spit making my guts ache.

I don't want to go under the spider's web bridge and I can't see the old church, but now there's a path with a signpost. I can't read what it says, but I think it must go up to the White walls at the top.

Hopefully I can find the old church and think that would be a good place to hide, but the path just goes to a garden which is underneath houses full of lights which I can't remember being there, so I huddle down in a hut.

I can't hear any voices although there is constant hum from the bridges and flickering lights like they're having a celebration or something?

But now I'm feeling a bit safer, my mind strays to thinking on my enemies and will they still be here? And what I'm going to do if I find them.

And then, Lord above, a package comes sailing down and lands not a yard a way, I can smell it's fish, so I scramble out, rescue it and quickly scrabble back.

It is fish? But in a strange covering, which is quite edible and then some pieces of soft vegetable, which I've never tasted before.

So, belly assuaged for now, I curl up in my coat and try to sleep, although my head is full of images of the town and places where I might be safe.

The last thing I remember is thinking when are they going to douse the lights?

CHAPTER TWELVE

In the event it's Anne who spots the binocular flashes across the other side of the valley.

At first she doesn't think anything of it, Helena had told her it was quite frequent, calling them 'nosy parkers' which sounds funny with her accent . . . but then she shivers, maybe they've already figured out where they are because of her.

Shaking, she rushes back in and bumps right into Tomasz, who is the last person she wants to tell . . . but she does.

He immediately finds his army issue high spec 'bins' and scans the road opposite . . . until he spots them.

He gives Anne a hug, which completely winds her, before he rushes off to find his rifle, shouting for Will on the way.

Plan made, he goes up on the roof, where there's cover all the way to the front crenelations. He's practised this shoot many times since he was a boy with a range of different weapons, but nothing so sophisticated as this weapon he'd commissioned from the army gunsmiths, which, of course, he should have given back when he was 'decommissioned'.

He gives Will the OK and then waits to see him driving his jeep down the drive, Dex in the passenger seat.

It's risky but the drive has trees all the way down to the houses below, so the potential shot would be as he stops at the main road.

Tomasz finds the target.

A Range Rover parked behind a bush . . . next to a tree.

Through the lens he can see the shooter's got a US rifle, which makes him laugh, as it was notoriously hopeless in Afghanistan.

He glances across at the drive and can see Will is going slowly and only half-way down.

Back at the target, the guy must have seen the jeep and now moved out of cover, so must have a death wish.

Tomasz lines him up.

Shoots.

Body blasted backwards.

He watches.

Second figure scuttles towards the vehicle.

Shoots.

He waits.

Tells Will, who is now down in the houses.

He continues to watch as Will makes his way over the bridge and up past the remains of Amelia's house and up to the Range Rover.

'Two men down,' comes the call.

Half an hour later, they're back at the house, Dex driving the Range Rover with the two bodies in the back.

It's at this moment that everyone realises that they are really in a war.

They search the two guys and their vehicle.

Apart from the usual 'two Americans abroad' clutter, they find a couple of phones and onboard GPS, which Will disconnected back where they were killed.

Sitting, but still hyped-up, Will wonders aloud.

'Not so bright, eh,' he murmurs.

Tomasz shakes his head.

'Um, they're just the first wave, send in the 'nutcases', they'll either take a few out but let you then know where the hardware is lurking.'

Dex nods.

'At least, we now know they know where we are.'

Tomasz makes a face.

'I was just trying to wing the second guy, but he ran too slowly.'

Will laughs.

'Bloody marksmen.'

Tomasz grins.

'Anyway, well done Anne!' he shouts and can feel the blushes through the wall.

But then Walker appears, Gill behind him.

He and Tomasz stare at each other.

Walker shrugs.

'Impressive, but . . .'

Tomasz shrugs.

'Feel free to tell your brass,' he sneers. 'I don't see them giving us any protection.'

Walker can only stare and shake his head.

'I can't imagine this guy is short of the funds to employ an army, if he wants to.'

Tomasz stares back.

Walker sighs.

'Ok, I'll see what I can do . . .'

Tomasz sighs.

'Do what you want but give Will some time to see if he can find out anything about the contacts on their phones. He's getting some info already although most of the orders are encrypted and coming from somewhere over the Atlantic, which suggests the husband is on his way . . . or more sophisticated operatives, rather than those two.'

Walker nods and looks at Gill, who makes a face saying, 'your call'.

Tomasz smiles.

'I understand, you know, I've been in your position many times. You can see what needs to happen, but the gormless, back behind the lines public school boys get all dithery when they have to make tough decisions.'

Walker can't help but smile.

But the standoff is interrupted by Helena declaring that dinner is ready . . . and no-one wants to ignore her.

*   *   *

It takes some time for them to calm Ellie down.

On the one hand she wants to find someone who can verify the coin, so Sybil's on the phone to the 'local know-it-all', but finds for once he's away in Edinburgh, not expected back till tomorrow.

And on the other hand she keeps getting flashbacks of the face peering at her from the church door.

'I need to go back,' she whispers, eventually.

Louisa and Sybil are both against this but then Fletcher says he'll go with her.

'I don't know whether I'll frighten him away,' he says, with a grin.

Ellie shakes her head.

'I hope not,' she whispers.

So the two 'sensible ones' wash their hands of them both and say they'll see them in the café down the road.

As it happens it's a grey day, rain threatening on and off, so there aren't many folk about as Ellie insists that they follow the wall to get to the 'Cowport' again, which Fletcher assumes must be what it was used for. They go down and he sees the Barracks are still closed.

They make their way to the church gates and Ellie shows him where she found the coin and the sunken gravestone.

Fletcher bends down to try to read the name but can't see anything.

'Are you sure this was the one?' he asks.

She nods and kneels down to get a better look, although she has to admit there's nothing legible.

They look at other near ones but there are no 'Nisbets'.

Ellie shivers and looks around.

'Are you searching for someone particularly?' says a voice.

They both turn to look, having to shade their eyes as he's standing with his back to the sun.

He comes towards them and they realise he's a monk in a black and white gown.

Ellie stares at him, telling herself he's a Benedictine. Fletcher stares at his sandals, no socks, thinking he must be freezing, although what does he know . . . but then he looks at Ellie and realises that she's trembling.

'Yes,' she stutters, 'I think there are members of my family buried here, called Nisbet.'

The man smiles.

'There are indeed, follow me,' he says and sets off past the main doorway and round the back of the church.

They follow, Fletcher realising Ellie's trembling with fear or excitement . . . or both?

The man stops near a big gravestone which tells them this is the grave of Cornelius Nisbet died 1797.

'One of the oldest,' the man murmurs.

Ellie nods.

'But I was told there was an older one,' she whispers.

The man frowns.

'No . . . not anymore.'

Fletcher can't quite see him properly as the sun is behind him again.

'In the terrible times after the dissolution many poor folk's graves were destroyed . . . their memories erased . . . forgotten . . . buried under the new walls by the evil English Kings' men. . . all the churches burned . . . thousands of people slaughtered, men women and bairns . . .' his voice angrier, but fading away . . .

Fletcher rubs his eyes.

Realises Ellie has fallen down.

He reaches down to her, goes on his knees.

Lifts her head, she's trembling, but breathing . . . he doesn't know whether to shake her or . . .

He looks up.

The man has gone.

Disappeared . . . 'into thin air.'

Ellie groans and her eyes flutter.

Gradually she recovers and sits up.

There's someone else.

A woman coming towards them.

'Are you alright?' she asks.

Gradually, Fletcher and the woman get Ellie onto her feet and take her into the church, where the woman comes with a glass of water.

'Did you see that man?' he asks.

The woman frowns.

'No . . .'

'He was a monk . . . Benedictine . . .' mutters Ellie.

The woman smiles.

'No, my dear, they're long gone, I'm afraid, not a nice story at all. Terrible times back in the day.'

Ellie nods.

'I know.'

The woman gives her a look.

'I'm a historian,' Ellie asserts, 'I know very well what happened here.'

The woman stares at her.

'Well . . . yes, of course, but . . . best not to dwell in the past, eh?'

Fletcher rolls his eyes.

'I shouldn't tell her that, you might get a long lecture or three.'

Ellie shakes her frown away.

'No, you're right,' she says to woman.

She's not too convinced but manages a smile and wishes them good day, before making a swift exit.

Ellie can't help but grin.

Fletcher shakes his head.

But any thoughts of finding the café are lost as she tells him they've got to go to St Nicholas and she sets off to the Cowport. He sighs and follows on; thinking isn't that Santa Claus and then wonders how he knows that?

*   *   *

Otka is frustrated, even shouted at Voudra on the phone, so Xavi just trails along after her, not knowing where they're going.

In the end he realises they're tailing Ellie, who Otka believes knows more than she realises, which makes two of them. She seems to be obsessed by the church round the wall and now she's got the old detective guy, Fletcher, following along with her.

Just now they were watching her from the car parked in front of the church where she found an old coin.

Otka whispers him to stay in the car while she creeps over to the hedge, but five minutes later she's rushing back and hiding behind another car, just as Ellie and Fletcher appear and march off towards the walls.

Otka waits till they head towards one of the tunnels under the wall and then gestures to him to follow them with her.
But then she scuttles back up on to the wall.

He follows and now they see the couple and the dog walking along a path, which is going back towards the estuary.

Except now they're going off the path between the two big humps towards what he now realises is a golf course! What? Really?

Otka tells him to continue on the wall until he can get down, while she'll go back and through the Cowport.

He watches as she runs away and then continues along the wall.

He can't see where the next exit is, but hurries along looking over to see if can see her.

In the event he sees an exit down a steep tunnel and scuttles down, through a gate, chooses right and comes up to a terrace of houses facing out over the estuary.

Not sure which way to go so he goes along behind the terrace, where he spots Ellie and Fletcher walking round the cricket pitch and then over to his left he sees Otka scurrying along through the humps.

It's at this moment all of them stop.

All he can see is ordinary, apart from the walls behind him, he could be anywhere on this coastline, even at home.

'Home'?

He's stung by the thought that their seaside hideaway is now their 'home' . . .

His eyes fill up and tears stream down his cheeks.

And it's then he sees the church.

Not big. No tower. But a lot of people . . . fighting? Screaming? Swords clashing? Bodies being stabbed?

But . . . then it's gone?

He rubs his eyes.

No, just the back of a terrace of houses, cars parked behind, a cricket pitch . . . no people apart from the girl and the man standing in the middle and Otka over to his left looking from the top of one of the humps.

What's going on?

*   *   *

URSULA

Janet is getting more and more restless. Walking along the river further and further each time . . . and as for conversation . . 'only if you want to tackle a bear with a sore head' as my mother used to say.

So I'm relieved when Ziggy asks where she is as he has something he'd like her to do.

I find her along by the river throwing stones at who knows what.

She shrugs but agrees to come back and go down to where Ziggy's ensconced.

I go to see what I can make for tea, then she arrives back upstairs.

'Don't bother about me,' she mutters, 'I'm being sent on an 'errand'.

I want to ask what? But . . .

'I've got to rescue Louisa and a friend, as she's fed up with being stuck in Berwick.'

I wait to hear if there's anymore, but she just makes a face . . . and she's gone.

Well, that means four of us, so I go to see what she has in her freezer and come back with a sizeable chicken and set about doing my mother's 'reserve' Sunday dinner.

But then I find myself staring out the window worrying about the two different situations being enacted elsewhere.

Ellie and Fletcher chasing ghosts while Tomasz and his gang await the arrival of the angry husband.

I only know little about both from snippets I get from Ziggy, not that he's telling me, just talking to himself when I take him food and drinks.

He's convinced the two situations are connected but hasn't enlightened me.

And all this to do with treasure stolen from way back when . . . Elizabeth the First . . . and of course, we didn't get that far before I dropped history to do cookery, which my mother said was far more useful than reading about Godless men fighting each other.

*   *   *

My intention was to go up to the top in the morning, where there's the western gate. . . no doubt well-guarded and me with no papers, meaning I have second thoughts as I didn't sleep well, so I venture back down to the river at first light.

It's a dull morning anyway and raining, so I decide to risk going under the spider's bridge seeing she doesn't seem to be clambering down here at all.

The old castle white walls are still there but it's even worse than I remember it. There are no guards down here and then there's a path going up, so I follow it . . . although it's a bit strange . . . there's a sign with writing and pictures on it which I can't understand because it's still dark and I don't want to be found here.

At the top I come out on a street I don't recognise and don't know which way to turn, but then I can hear the spider rattling along her threads so I go right and left and come to a road. I creep carefully towards it and peep out.

I don't remember shops this far outside the gate, but I can see it down to my right, so I hurry from one doorway to another and find the way up.

Also it's started raining so's it still quite dark.

I wait to see if there's any guards, but they don't seem to be any, although there are a few people walking up and down, but they don't seem to be bothered by me.

They're wearing strange clothing . . . and then there's a carriage coming. I dive into an entrance, it's past before I can see it, although the noise is strange . . . no horses?

Now I'm up the steps to the wall and lie low for a few moments.

It's very puzzling?

Why is the gateway wide open? And what's happened to the gates?

Well, I can't stay here, so I run along the wall. No guards?

Are they all dead. A plague?

I carry on and eventually come to the Cumberland Bastion, which again has no guards, not a soul?

I'm beginning to think I'm dreaming, but now I can see the Brass bastion, only recently finished - no guards, but . . . fairies? Lighting the way?

I go down the first steps as fast as possible, I'm not going to be bewitched . . . and find myself on a wide street . . . I go along by the walls and then come out in a huge space. A church on my left and then castle walls facing it.

There are some weird creatures lined up like huge rabbits, but they're still . . . sleeping?

I hurry past them and go into the graveyard and creep behind a gravestone and stop, trying to gather my breath.

It's starting to get light now, but I should be safe here . . . even though I don't remember this church here inside the walls? There was only St Nicholas and the tower wasn't safe.

As soon as I can get my breath, I scuttle across to the church door; thankfully it's not locked, so I'm in and sink down on the floor.

It's silent.

I stay still, listening for any people? Monks? Priests?

No one. I try to stop shivering but find that I'm weeping!

Not sure it's fear or relief I didn't get caught or challenged?

It's sometime later I come awake with a start.

Where am I?

It's dark, but some light coming through windows high up.

I remember.

I'm in a church.

Not one I know.

Can I stay here?

No-one's been in yet.

I don't know what day it is?

I don't even know what time it is?

I go to the door.

Normally church doors creak and groan, but this one doesn't.

I peep out.

Was that a dog barking?

I step further out.

I can hear someone rustling.

It's a girl . . . and a dog.
She's bending down, picking something up.
She stands up.
The dog leaps up at her. She's looking at what she's found on the ground.
She looks round, afraid.
I step back.
Wait.
She calls the dog.
I hear her running.
The gate clangs.
She's gone.
My heart is banging against my chest.
I go back and close the door.

CHAPTER 'THIRTEEN'

It's raining . . . again.

Xavi realises he's getting very wet.

Well, he is standing on a grassy hump staring at a cricket pitch . . . but where's the church? The one in flames? All the people running and screaming?

Then he sees a figure standing right in the middle of the pitch. Not a cricketer?

He's pretty certain that in the incomprehensible English game the 'players' all wear white?

No, it's Otka!

And now she's fallen down.

He stumbles down the hill and runs to her.

She starts to get up as he arrives, but then collapses again.

He kneels beside her and lifts her into his arms, she is so slight that he could pick up . . . he looks round for help.

But then she groans and her eyes flutter.

He calls her name.

Her eyes open, she frowns and struggles to sit up.

She stares at him.

He shakes his head.

But before she can say anything, there's Ellie and Fletcher running towards them.

A few minutes later they're all sitting together on a bench.

The conversation is stilted, all of them disturbed by what they think they might have seen and feeling awkward that the others will think them delusional.

But then there's voice calling them.

A woman waving at them.

It's Joan with her little dog.

'You'll be upsetting the cricketers,' she shouts.

Otka struggles to her feet, never liking being helped.

They go over to Joan, who sees Otka's a bit wobbly.

'Hey, come to my house – a cup of tea,' she orders.

So despite Otka being embarrassed by the fuss, they go out onto the road by the estuary and along to her house.

And now they're all sitting awkwardly, not wanting to share what they might have seen . . . which they're all thinking must have been a mirage.

'What were you doing out there?' asks Joan.

They shrug or shake their heads.

So, Ellie is the first to share, curious whether the others had seen the same thing.

'A church . . . on fire . . . people shouting, screaming, running . . .'

She stops, realising the others are staring at her, their own experiences probably matching hers.

She can't stop a smile.

'Not just me, then . . . for once.'

Despite this they're all a bit dumbstruck, which makes Joan even more puzzled.

'A church . . . you say . . . on fire?' asks Joan.

They all manage a few nods and embarrassed frowns.

But then Joan frowns as well.

'My, my,' she whispers . . , but then gets up and goes inside and comes back with a book and fingers the pages until she finds what she's looking for and passes it over to Ellie.

She reads and then gasps and looks up.

'There was a church, St Nicolas, in the fifteenth century. which some historians believe was on the site of the cricket pitch.'

The others stare at her.

'Demolished to make way for the Walls,' she reads.

'They knocked it down?' Fletcher can't help asking, knowing Ellie will know more than anyone else.

'Because it was Catholic,' she asserts.

Even Otka and Xavi know about the Reformation from dreary history lessons back home.

Joan shakes her head.

'I think you're right young lady,' she murmurs, 'terrible things done here back then.'

No-one else wants to add to this, so eventually the four of them thank her and set off.

Through the tunnel they say goodbye. Ellie and Fletcher heading back to the YHA, while Otka and Xavi set off to their flat, neither couple having a clue about what they're going to do next.

*   *   *

When the police come they show some respect for the family name, although more likely knowing Tomasz's reputation, which is what he's just recently confirmed. Just an unmarked car parking up at the stables and a transit van possibly jammed with eager beaver armed 'polis' down on the main road in full view.

Tomasz comes out on the terrace and waves them in.

Two chaps, probably Tulliallan's finest, smoothing their suits as they glide out of their car and come up the terrace like they'd been many times before.

He leads them through to his father's room, wishing he was there with him.

Suits smoothed again, the taller one smiles.

'DCI Kingston and DS Ross, sir.'

Tomasz nods, not about to outgun them with his rank and exploits.

He waits.

They shuffle.

'You're here about the incident yesterday,' he asserts, not wanting to beat any bushes.

Kingston smiles.

Tomasz doesn't.

'They're in the freezer, so I think you need to come back with a hearse.'

Kingston's smile vanishes and the hard look tells Tomasz why he was selected for this mission.

He waits.

'We understand that you were convinced they were going to 'attack 'you?'

Tomasz nods.

Kingston doesn't wriggle in his seat and there's a glimmer of a smile in his lips, but soon gone.

'He was waiting for my friends to get down to the main road. I saw him change his angle as they drove down.'

Again Kingston gives him time to elaborate, something Tomasz's record would have made clear : he never does.

'And the second man?'

'Same op.'

Kingston waits.

Tomasz smiles. Anyone who survived Afghanistan has patience burned in.

The silence gathers.

Ross gets tense.

Tomasz smiles at him.

'You don't need to worry, Sergeant . . . my gun is safely locked-up as per regulations.'

Kingston shakes his head.

'The problem is, sir, that we're not in Afghanistan here.'

Tomasz laughs.

'You think I don't know that?'

But then the steel hardens.

'You were told by the local police that this was possible . . . yet no response, no protection . . . so 'everyman's home is a castle' . . . especially here in the 'Rough Borders'.'

Kingston flinches.

'I understand your right to defend yourself . . . and your family . . . and friends, but the second one?'

Tomasz shakes his head.

'Always assume the second one is the better shot.'

Kingston frowns and looks away.

'If you're going to arrest me, you'll need more than a van full of squaddies and instead I think you should be investigating the American husband who's hiring, up to now, third rate assassins and kidnappers to retrieve his wife and daughters, who are terrified of him.'

Kingston stares at him.

'We are happy to provide protection for you and them, but there are . . . shall we say, legal arguments on his side.'

Tomasz stands up quickly, making the DS flinch.

He laughs at him, but then frowns.

'I think now's the moment you need to talk to his wife and daughters and see what they want to do.'

With that he strides out of the room.

Caught short the two officers quickly follow him.

He leads them to another room, where Catherine and her daughters are waiting.

The two parties stare at each other, Catherine determined not to cry and her girls stony-faced.

Tomasz introduces them and then stalks out.

It doesn't take long, so Catherine must have found some 'steel'.

The two suits nod on their way out, probably thinking having another conversation with Tomasz was above their paygrade.

Walker, Gill and the two ex-soldiers wait till they see the transit van disappear before coming back from where they were hiding.

Tomasz shrugs.

'I'm not holding my breath.'

The others concur and he goes to see Catherine.

The 'steel' is still there as he goes in, then she bursts into tears, but of anger not weakness.

'Damn 'polis',' she rasps, then has to laugh.

Tomasz gives her a hug.

'What did they say?'

She shakes her head.

'Apparently my 'husband' had told them we'd been kidnapped by 'Scottish Nationalist guerillas'!'

Tomasz can't help but laugh and then she's laughing as well.

He shouts for the others to come and hear.

So five minutes later they've run though all the possible leadership options of 'a SNP armed forces op', which reduces many of them to tears.

'What did the two suits think of that?' asks Gill.

'They tried to tell me that they knew that wasn't true, but that I should wonder why you had 'persuaded' us to come here.'

Tomasz frowns.

'So, did they tell you what they were going to do next?'

Catherine shrugs.

'Something like they'll have to 'reconsider their options'.'

Later, Tomasz and his 'guerillas' have a confab and whilst agreeing to continue what they're doing, decide Walker should see if he can talk some sense into his superiors.

He isn't exactly confident that he could but he said he'd try and got on the phone.

Just five minutes he comes back, shaking his head.

'Wankers,' he growls. 'I didn't get any further than my 'Super', who told me to 'come away', so I told him I was taking overdue leave and cut the call.'

Gill just nods 'me too'.

Tomasz goes to tell Catherine.

She shakes her head.

'I can't expect you all to put your lives on the line for me.'

Tomasz looks away.

'It's what we're trained for and we're used to it, don't worry.'

She can't help but smile.

Tomasz looks out the window.

'Have you tried contacting your husband?'

She nods.

'He's not responding . . . he thinks 'he knows best' . . . but I think it's more about the Elizabethan treasures than 'us'.'

Tomasz frowns.

'What do you mean?'

She sighs.

'I think he needs the money . . .'

Tomasz laughs.

'Are you serious?'

She nods.

'He thinks I don't know about his deals, thinks I don't understand 'business', but I've been running the estate for over twelve years, from when my first husband was still alive after he got dementia.'

Tomasz frowns again.

'So why did you marry him?'

She looks away.

He thinks she's going to cry, but then she looks back at him . . . no tears, just anger.'

'I fell for his charm, his talk about his money . . . which I now know were lies.'

Tomasz stares at her.

She glares back and then bursts into laughter, which ends in tears.

'I was such a fool,' she whispers.

And then her daughters come in and put their arms around her.

Tomasz shakes his head and thanks whoever blessed him with his parents.

*   *   *

Ellie doesn't know what to do.

While she knows Fletcher would defend her, he's the last person to believe in ghosts, so he thinks what he saw was some kind of delusion, although his heavy drinking days have passed and he's pretty certain all his marbles are in the right place.

She's given up trying to get some answers on the web, dismissing a lot of the fantasy stuff as witheringly as she has no truck with Tolkienesque dreams.

The archivist was helpful, but didn't give her much more than she already knew, so . . .

And no point in telling anyone about her sightings of 'ghosts' and figures disappearing round corners.

She fingers the coin in her pocket and pulls it out.

She's certain it's real.

The date is the period Lee was here, taking as much of Elizabeth's coins as he could.

And why can't she now find the gravestone she saw.

Who is Nisbet?

Who would know?

Henry **Grey** probably would, but that's no good . . . unless he left some other clues to where he hid the ruby necklace and the glass?

Rollo comes out from underneath her chair and put his paws on her knees.

She gives in. He's the only one who will always go for another walk and digging is something he's really good at, but then she knows the back way to Henry's and she has a key courtesy of his sister, although she doesn't think the solicitors know about that as Joan winked at her as she gave it to her and put her fingers to her lips.

So, thinking Fletcher's happy enough in the café downstairs chatting up old ladies, she sneaks out the back door into the alley and straight away she sees someone disappearing up at the end?

She frowns.

She runs to the end and looks both ways. Where has she seen that figure before. A very thin person?

It's only a five-minute run to Henry's, even if she doesn't go on the wall, because she's figured out a shorter route, with more corners, so five minutes she's shutting the door to Henry's back garden and then quickly uses the key..

Inside Rollo is excited and woofles around the big rooms and then scuttles up the wide staircase, which Henry probably wouldn't have liked.

She stands listening to the house settling even though Rollo's sniffling around upstairs.

Where would a man who liked the excitement of selling stolen goods hide them?

Probably not under the floorboards like his phone.

She looks out the window.

People passing by on the walls oblivious to what she was doing . . . which always gives her a buzz.

It's only then she hears someone downstairs! Didn't hear them come in.

She creeps out onto the landing and sneaks a peek down to find herself staring at Otka looking up at her.

They both can't stop gasping and then giggling.

She goes down to find it's both of them, Xavi shaking his head.

'What are you doing in here?' he asks.

'Same as us, I suspect,' says Otka.

Ellie can't help but shrug.

'But where?' she asks.

Otka shakes her head.

'No idea, but to be honest, I don't think here.'

Ellie frowns.

'So where . . ?'

Otka shrugs.

'Got to start somewhere.'

The three of them wander upstairs.

Find themselves in what was his business room, shelves of books covering a wide range of precious objects from all over the world.

His desk is clear. No clues there.

'Look at these,' says Ellie, fingering a book on a middle shelf. 'He's got hundreds of books about the Tudor period.'

They stand together, Otka shaking her head.

Ellie pulls one out and opens it.

'Aha,' she laughs, thinking how outraged Louisa would be. 'He turns the page corners in.'

Otka and her quickly start opening different books to look at the turned down pages.

Xavi shrugs, his English isn't as good as hers, but then he sees one book which is sticking out a bit more than the rest on its shelf.

He lets it open where it wants and gasps.

'Hey,' he whispers, 'look.'

He holds it up open at the page which has a photograph.
. . . a necklace of red jewels.'

Both the girls have to put their hands over their mouths to stop screaming out loud.

But then Otka grasps it from him.

'It's definitely Queen Mary's necklace,' she murmurs, recalling the unexpected heaviness in her hand.

'So where . . ?'

'Lets' go back to talk to Joan again,' murmurs Ellie, 'she might know more than she's said . . . or something she doesn't realise she knows.'

*   *   *

URSULA

Janet comes back up from the cellar, a frown on her face.

'Ziggy's got a plan, which means I've got to go to some place beyond Tomasz's house.'

I've never been there, although I have seen it from the riverbank high up on the hillside, mostly hidden by fir trees . . . and I had a quick tour online courtesy of Ziggy, which made me dizzy – hundreds of rooms.

She tells me the plan is to make the American think they're going back to Edinburgh, but it's just a trick to get them elsewhere.

So she has to go and pick them up and take them to Berwick, where Ziggy's negotiating a safe house with someone.

As usual this is all too much cloak and dagger and I'd rather be in the kitchen.

But now it's for real.

Janet says she's hired a car and it'll be here any minute, so she's stuffing things into her rucksack . . . including something wrapped in a scarf . . . which I suspect is her gun.

So when she's saying goodbye at the door I run and hug her . . . which probably shocks me more than her.

163

*   *   *

Tomasz took some persuading, but in the end Ziggy's plan was clever enough and even if the stepfather thinks it's suspicious he won't be able to ignore it.

But the best part was that the trick was to get Mary to set it, by sending a message to her stepfather.

The hardest part was persuading Walker and Gill to play the diversionary tactic, taking Mary's phone with them so the father thinks he's tracking her.

Out the back of the house, up to the top of the hill, there's a small road going north, which goes all the way to a station at Stow where you can catch a train to Edinburgh . . . which is where the two detectives are going to drive to, while Becket will come and pick Catherine and the girls up and take them on a different road through Galashiels to Berwick, where Ziggy has organised a safe house.

So that's the plan for tomorrow morning . . . early.

*   *   *

RALPH

I don't seem to need much sleep, but then I never did, always at someone's beck and call.

So I wait till it's very dark and when I step outside I can't hear anyone.

I noticed that there was a gate in the wall in the graveyard, so I'm soon through and up towards the top of the wall, but then there's some fairies again so I go back.

There seems to be a lot more streetlights than I remember, which must cost a fortune, but it means I can see my way around the graveyard, even though there are none in here. I go to where I saw

164

the girl find the coin and see the sunken gravestone she was looking at.

I finger the name.

N - I - S - B - E - T

Nisbet?

Why is that familiar?

Do I know someone with that name?

I can't see the date?

But it's getting brighter now and I can see there's a castle gate over the wall. Don't remember that?

I think I'm better off in the church, until I can find someone to talk to.

CHAPTER FOURTEEN

Not many people get much sleep in the big house, maybe only Tomasz and Imelda, who did the midnight to the four stretch, but still up and ready by seven.

So Walker and Gill set off at eight, with Mary's phone and the back full of Gill's dad's armoury all present and correct, followed by Will and Dex as backup.

But it's not much later that Becket arrives and not wanting to have more than a quick brew, she's hustling the girls and their mother into her Landrover.

This means there's not much more than a few kisses with the remaining gang, now back down to its original occupants.

Nothing much is said for the whole journey to Berwick; Becket never up for 'conversation' or the 'state of the weather'.

Back at the house Tomasz and his mother give some thought to facing any last-minute attacks, while Imelda keeps watch.

Sticking to the plan, Tomasz phones the village police number knowing it will be transferred to Galashiels.

And tells them there's a gang with a shedload of guns, definitely not for shooting at grouse, on the minor road a couple of miles south of Stow, then ending the call abruptly with some shouting.

He knows that Walker and Gill and their following support will have taken the cut through at the bridge and now zooming up the main road.

He reckons the words 'guns' will trigger an armed response unit so they'll probably be there before the ambushers figure out what's happened and rush north to the station.

He's also been in touch with Kirsty, who has the village pub, to tell her what's about to happen, as he knows it'll be round the village in minutes and plenty of guns available.

So now he's sitting on the terrace, no vehicles in sight and waits for the first calls.

*   *   *

Despite the adrenaline running through his body Walker is wondering how this latest escapade will go down with his superiors. He glances at Gill, who returns the look, indicating she's thinking the same things.

She shrugs.

'Going out with a bang,' she mutters.

As it happens it's more like a Mad Hatter's tea party.

They are the first to arrive, so they pull up behind the new station building. There must be a train expected as there's quite a few folk standing around with miserable 'going-to-work-morning-faces' or fingering their phones trying to contact anyone else up so early.

'Didn't think about that,' mutters Walker; the last thing he wants is a massacre of innocent commuters.

Gill shrugs, thinking they might like a bit of mayhem for once in their dreary lives.

The time stumbles by, perhaps wondering if the next people on stage have forgotten their lines, but the reality is more farce than tragedy.

One of the people waiting stands up, somehow knowing the train is nearly here, a few others look down the line.

But then their attention is arrested by the sight of two 'army' lorries coming hell for leather along the lane above the station, which makes a couple of them smile and shake their heads knowing the level crossing gates have already closed.

Most of them are now watching to see what the lorries do and then see them skid to a halt and soldiers jumping out . . . with guns?!

167

But even then they don't get to do much panicking or running away, because behind them a slew of police cars and a van are disgorging an equal number of armed police officers.

No shots get fired because the train carefully intervenes causing consternation for all three teams.

Orders can be heard from both sides of the train, while the platform commuters don't know whether to run or get on the train, but the most puzzled are the people already on the train.

They gradually realise the regulars are scuttling about instead of queuing at the doors and then they see the guns on both sides!! Some of them just stare, others start screaming and getting into the aisles.

As time slows down, the would-be kidnappers lose their bottle first, turning and running back to the lorries.

The police realise this and two groups go either side of the train and start firing into the air.

An officer with a loud hailer urges them to put their guns down and then the men in the trucks realise another couple of police vehicles have come up the lane behind them.

The rest of the event is a bit of a disappointment, although the commuters have the eventual rest of the journey to concoct much more colourful tales to tell their disbelieving workmates and block a lot of people's phones with not very exciting images of police putting handcuffed 'soldiers' into vans.

The event only gets a small mention on news programmes, after the police asserted it was just a minor operation, no-one was hurt.

Having informed both Tomasz and Becket the 'op' was successful, Walker and Gill can't help laughing as they go into the village to meet up with Will and Dex at Kirsty's, where the villagers are all talking at once, They didn't even get interviewed, plenty of other willing witnesses, all of them embellishing their 'involvement' more and more as they retell it.

*   *   *

Becket passes on the news to Catherine, who is relieved no-one got hurt, but nervously wondering where she and the girls are going next, her nerves not helped by Becket's aggressive driving.

But it means the journey is over quickly and they're pulling up in a back street in Berwick.

Becket manages a smile with the two girls as she helps them with their luggage.

Although it's not until they're safely inside that the girls realise they're right on the walls, huge windows looking out at the estuary.

'Wow,' says Mary.

Becket goes though into the kitchen to find the delivery Ziggy ordered has arrived so she sets to, making a brew and finding some biscuits.

Now she's telling Ziggy they're installed and asking if there's any more news?

'Only that I've blocked their phones and credit cards, new ones on the way.'

She finds Catherine staring out the window at the sea, so she offers her the mug and stands next to her.

Catherine gives her a weak smile and whispers 'thank you'.

Becket lets the silence gather; she knows it works.

Then she tells her about the cards and phones.

'Oh, the girls won't like that,' she murmurs.

Becket shakes her head.

'I'll tell them, they must know by now that we're trying to keep them safe.'

'You must think I'm stupid,' Catherine whispers.

Becket shakes her head.

'Men are 'bastards' . . . in my experience and the one thing they have of any use can be acquired otherwise.'

Catherine checks to see if she's joking, but the hard face says no.

At which point there's someone shouting through the letter box.

Becket grins.

'Although there are few exceptions,' she mutters and she goes to let him in.

*   *   *

Ellie and her two new 'compadres' find Joan sitting out in the little front garden, chatting with someone who's on the way back from the beach.

But she soon goes in to get them a drink, none of these three drinking coffee or tea.

Ellie gives the other two a wink and goes after her to offer help.

She glances into the front room, which is 'old lady' pristine, no books in sight, although she is surprised to see one of Lowry paintings she said she didn't like on the wall.

Down the corridor she makes the old lady jump, but it just makes her laugh.

'Not used to people in here,' she giggles, 'good job I did the washing up.'

Ellie thinks it looks like the kitchen's just been installed.

But she takes the tray and follows her back outside.

So now Otka and Xavi once again feel awkward with this English old lady behaviour, but if they were honest their grandmothers are just the same.

And it's Ellie who expertly moves the conversation to Joan's brother.

'So . . . ' she asks, 'have you decided to keep at least one of the Lowrys?'

Joan frowns.

'I saw it in the mirror as I came along,' adds Ellie with an apologetic smile.

'Well . . .' Joan blushes, 'if he went to all that trouble not selling them for himself, I thought I'd keep one of them.'

Ellie nods.

'Do you think I could have a proper look at it?'

Joan shrugs.

'Of course.'

So the two of them go to the front room and look at it.

It's his usual style, wobbly walls and one thin figure at the end of the passage.

Ellie frowns at it.

First, because she thinks it's like one she's seen in a book and secondly because it is so like the figures she's seen recently flitting away from her.

'Do you know where it's supposed to be?' she asks.

Joan shrugs.

'Could be anywhere, lots of little 'wynds' like that round here.'

Ellie can't help giving the painting another glare.

Back outside the sun's come out from behind the clouds and the estuary is shimmering in their eyes.

'I'm lucky to live here,' whispers Joan.

Ellie nods, but she's thinking about the figure . . . or rather all the figures, Lowry's paintings filled with them, not just here, but all his paintings mostly back near his home in Salford.

They sat in silence for a few minutes.

'You do know he once wanted to buy the 'Lions house',' Joan murmurs.

'What?' asks Ellie.

'You weren't far from it when you were playing about on the cricket pitch.'

Ellie frowns trying to think what the wall is like just there.

'If you go back through the tunnel from here and turn right up onto the walls and keep going to the top of the hill it's on your left. A big house with two stone lions on its gateposts.'

Ellie can't believe that she didn't know this.

'So why didn't he buy it?'

Joan shrugs.

'I think it needed a lot of work doing. It was empty for years, but somebody bought it recently and did it up.'

So inevitably she has to go and look and there it is, she'd obviously always been looking out to sea on that stretch.

*   *   *

Louisa is in a strange mood, doesn't seem to be able to rest. One minute she's in the sitting room, then she appears in the kitchen and then I hear her standing at the doorway to 'Ellie's' room, which produces some loud tuts and what I think are called 'harrumphs'.

But now she's come back to the kitchen where I'm trying to sort an evening meal.

'That girl,' she mutters, 'she needs to tidy 'her' room up . . . it's actually 'my' library!

But then she shakes her head and burst into tears.

As I've never seen her cry, I'm astounded. Don't know what to do or say, having been brought up by a mother who regarded crying as almost a sin.

And this is Louisa, the strongest person I've ever known.

And far too scary for me to even thinking of putting my arm around her, so I have to pretend I didn't hear or see this outburst.

I try to concentrate really hard on peeling the potato in my hand until I realise I've already peeled it.

I peep over my shoulder.

She's gone?

I put the potato down and creep out after her.

Can't find her?

Then realise where she'll be.

Sure enough she's in the conservatory, standing looking out towards the river.

I venture in . . . no idea what to do or say.

It seems an age but only a few seconds.

'Well, there's a thing,' she murmurs and then blows her nose.

I wait, trying not to breathe.

'Louisa 'Virginia' Cunninghame crying?'

Now she's turning round and laughing.

'If you ever tell anyone I'll have to kill you,' she says in a voice more like her usual, but then she laughs again.

I still don't know what to do or say.

But then the most extraordinary thing happens.

She walks up to me and puts her arms round me and hugs me so tight I can hardly breath.

And then she kisses full on the lips.

And then pushes me away.

I'm paralysed with . . . fear? No, just astonishment.

No! Disbelief!

She laughs again.

'Actually I don't care,' she mutters, 'and you're safe, I'm not going to invite you into my bed, I have enough trouble dealing with that old duffer Fletcher, thank you very much!' and then she laughs again.

She grins at me,

'Gin and tonic, I think, and what's for tea? I'm starving.'

The only thing that makes me smile later is 'Virginia'?

And no, I won't tell a soul!

*　　　*　　　*

RALPH

I'm getting a bit weary of only going out in the dark, but until I can find out who's in charge, the English or the Scots, I think I'm best lying low.

This church is strange, I think it must be Protestant, although the altar has a lot of gold and tapestries.

There's also a weird section on the left of the nave, which is full of flickering lights like moths and fireflies, so I keep away from it.

But most of the time it's empty, apart for the services which are what I expected, although they're not very well attended and most of the congregation are old, spending a lot of the time at the end whispering to each other like they're telling secrets.

I wouldn't know because they're not talking English . . . although I hear a few English words . . . and Scottish accents.

But now it's quiet. I think I heard a key being turned in the lock . . . meaning I'm safe for the night, I suppose.

CHAPTER FIFTEEN

It isn't a surprise that when Walker and Gill excuse themselves and set off back, to find there's a black van blocking them in and a Mercedes next to it.

The guys in the van give them a hard stare and then a 'chap' in a suit gets out of the Merc and nods at Walker as he opens the back door.

He gets in, giving Gill a wink.

She gives the suit a sneer and goes to sit on a nearby wall turning away to look down the valley.

She reckons ten minutes tops, but it's actually nearly half an hour when Walker gets out, trying not to grin.

She looks at the suit who gives her a raised eyebrow and a shake of his head, before he gets back in the car and it swishes away, heading to Galashiels.

The van after it.

Walker nods at the jeep and they get in.

She waits, telling herself she doesn't care and can do without the grief anymore.

But then Walker's grinning.

'Well, that's the softest bollocking I've ever had.'

Gill frowns but then can't help grinning herself.

'He even reckons we might get a commendation but not to hold our breath . . . upstairs not liking the 'off-piste' behaviour.'

She has to laugh.

They both find their bodies relaxing.

'But what about the wife and daughters?'

He shrugs again.

'I told them they were alright, still at the house with their brother.'

'What do they think about him?'

Walker shakes his head.

'I think they know about him, but they didn't say anything, so I'm just giving him a heads up, although I suppose he's expecting a visit.'

The call is brief.

'So what now?' she asks.

He shrugs.

'He didn't explicitly say we couldn't return, so . . .'

Gill makes a face.

'Meaning?'

'Maybe he likes the idea of 'off-piste officers' in this situation and he intimated they were investigating the husband.'

Gill sits back staring out the window.

'But you didn't tell them about the removal?'

Walker smirks.

'He didn't ask me.'

She looks at him.

He shrugs again.

'I don't know.'

Gill sighs and turns on the engine.

She nods at the pub, which is still doing a roaring trade, alcohol making the witnesses 'experiences' more and more extravagant, no doubt reaching up to Bond style interventions etcetera.

She decides to go back the way they came via the cut through, both of them wondering what to do next.

*　　*　　*

Becket opens the door.

'How the hell did you know we were here?' she demands.

Fletcher pushes past her.

'Where's the loo?'

She points upstairs and sighs.

'Men.'

'Women!' comes the response.

She goes to put the kettle on again.

He reappears.

'Who do you think?' he asks.

But Becket just nods.

'Ziggy.'

'So where's Ellie?' he asks.

Becket shrugs.

'I thought that was your job?'

Fletcher accepts the mug of coffee.

'Yeh, well, one minute she's there and then she's disappeared. . . off grid.'

Becket checks her phone and turns the search on. She had an ex-colleague who put on an off grid tracking app for her, which she uses to keep tabs on people, particularly Ellie, who's the one who's always disappearing.

'Actually, not far away, just the other side of the wall.'

She hesitates, not sure Ellie's phone is that safe.

'It would be a good idea if you go and get her.'

'Just got here,' he moans.

'Well, it's only five minutes away.'

Glugging the coffee, down and then looking at Becket's phone, he grumbles out the door and away.

She goes back to Catherine.

'It's like herding cats,' she announces.

Catherine frowns.

Becket laughs.

'That was Fletcher, I just realised where Ellie is and so he's gone to fetch her.'

Catherine gives her a worried look.

'It's OK,' says Becket, 'Ellie's phone is Ziggy protected, like mine.'

Catherine shakes her head.

'Who is this Ziggy person?'

'Ah . . .' mutters Becket . . . 'you're better not knowing . . . just think . . .' but then she's stuck for a description. 'Spider' comes to mind, but that makes her shudder.

Five minutes later Ellie and Fletcher appear.
Ellie says 'hello', but then calls Ziggy.

'Three things,' she says.
'One, did you know about the Magazine and two the Lions house?'
'Yes,' comes the one-word reply, 'and three?'
'Why did Lowry paint 'stick men' . . . and is there a connection between them and ghosts?'
'Ghosts?'

Ellie hesitates, she doesn't want to talk to him about ghosts on the phone, she needs to see his face.
'No, actually, it's four. Do you think Henry knew a lot about Lowry? Is it worth thinking that he might hide the cache in a Lowry painting site?'
No response.
She waits.
What does this mean?
'Are you there?'
'Um,' says Ziggy, 'I'll get back to you on that . . . interesting idea.'
Frustratingly he cuts the call.

She stands looking out the window, but not at the view. Then she fingers her phone to find the Lowry trail site and quickly figures out which places would have been there in the sixteenth century.
She stops, thinking Ziggy will be doing the same searches, but can't help herself and continues.
It doesn't take her long, because she deletes most of them, either because the sites are no longer the same or not within the walls, which leaves her with four 'probables' and decides to go

straight away tipping her head at Fletcher . . . the pair of them sneaking out without telling anyone.

*   *   *

The black Mercedes purrs down the drive and pulls up at the edge of the terrace.

Tomasz is waiting on his own after the call from Walker, thinking they still might not know about Will and Dex who have returned and now hiding indoors.

Two suits get out, dark glasses, like they're American gangsters . . . which makes him shake his head. No idea whether they're the same gang as the previous ones or they've no confidence in their ability to communicate with each other.

He waits.

He doesn't have a gun with him but knows there are four behind him.

A third man now gets out and makes a show of looking at the view, before making his way up the steps to him.

Tomasz reluctantly shakes his hand and offers him a seat but nothing else.

He waits.

'I don't think I've met anyone who has personally killed over three hundred people and not in jail,' the man says softly.

Tomasz smiles, no intention of rising to such a blatant bait.

Another long pause.

'The thing is . . . we can't have people defending themselves in such a manner.'

Tomasz shakes his head.

'As I said to one of your 'men', if you won't, I will.'

Now the man shakes his head.

Another long stalemate.

'We understand that, but we can't allow it,' the man eventually says.

Tomasz sighs.

The man shakes his head again.

'I need to talk to Mrs Turnbull?'

Tomasz sighs.

'Well, in the first place, she's 'Lady' Turnbull and secondly, she's not here.'

The man smiles.

'I'm sorry, 'Lady' Turnbull . . . but I do have to ask if we can 'confirm' that.'

Tomasz smiles again.

'Are you calling me a liar, sir?'

The man smiles back.

'I'm not so sure you're so good a marksman at close quarters?'

Tomasz stares at him.

'Do you want to test that theory?'

The man smiles again.

'However . . .' rasps Tomasz, 'if you can come back with a court order, I may relent, although I think my lawyers will need to know what evidence you have that this woman and her daughters are hidden here.'

The man sighs.

But it is at this moment that, against Tomasz's orders, his sister and mother appear.

They introduce themselves as a retired local DI and a highly decorated WW2 resistance fighter in such a strident manner that Tomasz has to look away at the fierce look his mother is giving this man, which he can't return.

Five minutes later he's gone.

It's only then that the Will and Dex appear both trying to stop laughing.

Tomasz picks up his phone and makes the call to the solicitor as they'd agreed, but can't give him any names, so he says he'll make some enquiries, but will also immediately begin the legal action they'd agreed about harassment and a lack of official papers or identification.

It's not in Otka's nature to trail round after someone else, especially someone so young, although Ellie does seem to be very sure of herself . . . and more importantly she seems to know all the people involved . . . except Henry.

So when she comes down the steps, she gives her a questioning look.

Ellie shrugs, she prefers working on herself, but these two have the same questions, particularly 'where has Henry hidden the stolen goods?'.

'There's a house not far from here that Lowry wanted to buy, but it needed too much work to do,' she tells them, thinking it's hardly a secret.

Otka frowns.

'Lowry?'

'Ah,' says Ellie, thinking how she can explain him, but then fingers her phone and shows them some of his paintings.

Otka is still puzzled.

'So this 'artist' lived here?'

Ellie shakes her head.

'He came lots of times because he liked painting here . . . but he lived in Manchester . . . he's famous.'

Otka looked at her phone again.

'They're strange, like a child would do?'

Ellie shrugs.

'Look at the people?' Otka shows Xavi, who grins.

"Matchstick men',' he nods. 'I read it somewhere.'

'Yeh, there's going to be an exhibition here in a few weeks,' says Ellie, who's now getting impatient.

'Listen if you want to come with me I'm going to check out the house.'

Otka nods and they set off.

It's only two minutes away.

Ellie strides up the pathway to the door and knocks.

No answer, but then an old man clad in overalls comes round from behind the house, .

'They're not here,' he grumbles.

Ellie frowns.

'Do you know when they'll be back.'

He shrugs.

'Dinna say . . . but if you're going to break in, I wouldn't try if I was you – more alarms than a bank.'

Ellie laughs.

He grins and shuffles off.

They go back down to the gate.

Ellie wonders what to do, although she doesn't want these two following her all over the place.

'Listen,' she says, thinking she's getting more like Louisa every day, 'I've some private things to do, so I'll see you in the YHA café later,' and sets off along the walls.

She doesn't look back until she's nearly at the Barracks and is relieved to see that they've disappeared.

So now she takes out her little list of the possible Lowry trail paintings spots. The nearest is Strother Lane, but her map doesn't have it, so she figures out where it must be.

*   *   *

Becket is a bit fed up with this.

Being on 'potential victims watch' was never her favourite posting. She was happier going after the suspected villain, although in this case the villain is on a plane somewhere over the Atlantic according to Ziggy, so beyond her reach anyway. And she suspects he won't personally appear anyway until his wife and daughters have been 'recovered' from whoever has 'kidnapped' them.

So his whereabouts are irrelevant in one sense, but knowing who he might be sending to retrieve them, who could already be here and could turn up any time is a big worry.

She calls Ziggy.

Unusually he responds immediately.

'I've managed to find the 'people' who the husband has 'engaged to rescue' his family . . . '

'And?' she asks impatiently.

Another wait.'

'Um, not good,' he murmurs.

'Four of them . . . I've got background on three of them, ex-Afghan special forces etcetera . . . as far as I can tell they just didn't want to stop killing people and now available . . . but, shish! . . . not cheap!'

Becket now very worried.

'So what do you suggest?' she asks.

There's a long pause.

'Um . . . I've got a few contacts with the possible ability to engage . . . I'll get back to you.'

Becket sighs and puts away her phone.

Taking on Afghan vets not something she wants to do and certainly Fletcher and Ellie not able to take them on, in fact seriously at risk, so . . .

*　　　*　　　*

Tomasz is still cross with his sister and mother . . . but now gets a call from Ziggy, who tells him about the Afghan vets.

Tomasz sighs.

'Any idea when?' he asks.

'Not sure but arriving UK in the next twelve hours or so.'

Tomasz looks across at Will, who is frowning back at him.

He ends the call and nods Will out onto the terrace.

Dex is already out there and the three of them discuss the situation.

Will eventually shakes his head.

'We need to tell the guys who were here just now,' he says.

Tomasz shrugs.

'What do we tell them?'

Will looks away.

'Suppose we could ring round try to get some of the old boys to a party?'

Tomasz can't help but smile, recalling the shindigs they've had in the past, although the memories are understandably patchy.

But then he shakes his head.

'I don't think so, if they're like some of the Americans who were supposed to be on our side, I wouldn't trust them to be sober or clean never mind psychotic weirdos.'

Will looks away and sighs.

The three of them stand there, nightmares resurrecting themselves in broad daylight.

Tomasz yells to the sky. Not a distinguishable word, just a scream of anguish.

But then he turns on his heel.

The other two glance at each other and follow him, Will just catching the final few words spat out as he strides away . . . something like 'if they want a fight, I'll . . .'

When they get inside he's standing at the window, an old mobile in his hand . . he waits and the call is answered.

There's a lot of 'old bastards' and 'yeh of course you dids', but then he's giving them the scenario.

This goes on for a good hour or so as he goes through the alphabet on the phone.

Eventually he sighs and puts the phone on the balustrade.
Will gives him a look.
Tomasz grins.
'I think we might have a 'dirty dozen' or so, including us.'
Will grins.
Dex shakes his head at the thought of who they might be.

*   *   *

184

I'm thinking going out in the dark will be safer so I go to find if there's another door which isn't locked.

Eventually I find a little door which is off the sanctuary, but it's locked as well.

Frustrated I push at it . . . and my hand goes through it!

I stare at it!

My hand is *in* the door?!

But no pain?

I pull it back.

It doesn't hurt . . . and my hand isn't bleeding??

I try again.

It goes in . . . I keep going . . . right through into the room!!!

Did that really happen?

Am I dreaming?

I look around.

As I thought, it's the vestry.

Priests' vestments hanging in a wardrobe.

But what just happened?

I try again . . . going through the door and back into the chancery!

What does it mean?

And then it hits me!

I'm a ghost!

CHAPTER SIXTEEN

Once the decision is made Tomasz goes into captain mode, giving orders to all the others.

This is fine with Will and Dex who are used to him, although his sister and mother are less biddable, both having different views about defensive arrangements. Magda because she's used to having the backing of a full army of colleagues, which she can no longer count on, while Helena is getting some powerful flashbacks of running the streets in Warsaw.

One good thing is that her husband had accrued a room full of weapons and ammunition, more for slaughtering the local wildlife than villains, but nevertheless plenty enough for this battle.

And then there's the substantial stock of fireworks, because he loved a big display for any excuse. They wouldn't hurt the enemy very much but they would be excellent for disorientating them.

So now they're all busy making sure they're ready to defend attacks from any direction, although the only viable one is from the top of the hill through the trees, which means Tomasz and Will are setting traps and explosive devices. Dex has been given the job of supplies for the defence of the terrace.

Magda is on the phone getting different sorts of supplies, while Helena insists on manufacturing a huge amount of Molotov cocktails using her husband's enormous wine cellar, which she says they're never going to drink them because most of them have given up alcohol.

The only person not busy is Imelda, who self-appointed herself as lookout and went up on the roof, where she's distributed some of the guns and ammunition. Tomasz has recovered some old headsets and has hooked her up to his phone.

Walker and Gill reluctantly decided to join in with these almost certainly illegal activities, choosing not to inform their superiors, although he suspects they're worried enough to be doing something behind the scenes.

So after all this activity, mid-afternoon finds most of them on the terrace having a late lunch.

Much of this work has been done with the minimum of conversation, and now there's an eerie silence.

But not for long.
Tomasz gets a call from Imelda.
'Vehicle coming up to you,' she says.
Tomasz stands at the edge.
An old Commer van struggling up the hill?
But then he's looking through his binoculars and laughs.
'I thought he was dead!' shaking his head.

Two minutes late the van coughs to a stop by the stables and three people tumble out.

*   *   *

URSULA

Louisa and I are trying to stay calm, but knowing mayhem is about to erupt everywhere and hoping Ziggy can either confuse or delay the bad guys.

But for now we're sitting in the conservatory drinking tea and eating homemade scones, one of my few reasonably edible culinary achievements.

This room is always restful, even though with the outside doors open there are a few bees and flies drawn in by the heady perfume of Louisa's numerous exotic flowers, whose names I can never remember.

'Remind me again how we got ourselves involved with this band of ruffians?' she asks, a slight smile on her face.

Caught on the hop, I'm initially at a loss.

How and when indeed?

But before I can cast my mind back, the house phone rings.

Two questions.

One: who uses actual phones anymore? Even I've got an old mobile Ziggy gave me, although I rarely use it.

And two: where is it?

Louisa frowns, realising the nearest house phone is back in the kitchen.

She gives me a look.

I know my place and go to find it.

It's a man's voice.

'Hello, can I speak to Louisa Cunninghame, please.'

I hesitate. Ziggy, and all the recent events, have made me much more suspicious.

'Who can I say is calling? ' I ask, somehow finding my office voice from a long time ago.

There's no pause.

'A friend of her late husband, we never met, but she might remember my name, Neil Prentice.'

I certainly haven't heard that name, so the office response kicks in.

'Actually, I think she's on another call, so if you give me your number, I'll get her to call you back.'

'No, that's ok, I'll try again later.'

The phone clicks.

But even my docile sense of danger kicks in.

I go quickly back to Louisa, who is holding her mobile to her ear.

'No,' she says, 'never heard of him.'

She looks at me with her stern face, which would silence a whole room of people, so I just freeze.

She listens, murmurs something and cuts the call.

I'm still frozen.

Her blue gaze turns me ten degrees colder.

But then she grins.

'Well, done,' she whispers.

I don't understand.

'Ziggy says he only just caught it, as he'd forgotten about the landline.'

I shake my head.

'Anyway, he says he's got a tag on the phone and said it was from Heathrow.'

'So , who . . ?' I whisper.

Louisa sighs.

'According to Ziggy 'the vulture has landed', which I assume is his nomenclature for the 'bad guy'.'

I'm trying not to frown at her choice of words, as much as his, but getting the gist.

'However,' Louisa continues, getting up and smoothing her dress, 'if he thinks I'm going to wait here for some American thugs to turn up and trash my house, he doesn't know me as well as I thought he did.'

It's one of those moments I fear, when the speed of events leaves me stranded, not knowing what to do.

'Come on,' she orders, 'you and me are going on holiday.'

With that she strides to the door and I hear her going upstairs.

I run after her, wondering where we're going to disappear to . . . and who's going to look after Ziggy?

It was only a half an hour or so, as if I'd actually asked her, she told me in the car.

'Two 'very nice' Polish girls, apparently,' she said, 'although not what you're thinking, it's their combative skills he's hiring them for . . . he said . . . skills honed in Ukraine and elsewhere . . . and I've told the police I've had threatening phone calls and am going away for a few days. '

I'm thinking that's still not necessarily protecting the house, but she seems to be alright with it, so . . . and I wasn't thinking what she thought I was thinking . . . but I am now!

*   *   *

Becket is telling herself it's not as bad as it looks . . . but failing.

Why is she still getting herself into such nightmare situations? She's nearly at retirement age, certainly way beyond police retirement, but she's putting it off, while Ziggy seems to be able to keep paying her, which no-one else knows about . . . and she's not even there! Apparently he's now employing a couple of Polish 'cleaners'!

Well, it was never sex between them, especially as he wasn't bothered what gender you might be sex wise, which she didn't like.

So she is doing protection! Again!

Women? OK? But teenagers, who seem to be genetically connected to their mobiles are a nightmare. And taking them off them like tearing a limb off . . . and now doing Olympic level sulking.

And if that wasn't enough, she's got Fletcher and Ellie as 'helpers'?!

So she needs to put down some rules and gathers them all together apart from Ellie who she's posted on lookout.

It doesn't go well.

Mary sitting with her back to her.

Anne sullenly looking at her hands and their mother trying not to cry.

But then it's Fletcher who sorts it out.

'I tell you what, 'sergeant',' he murmurs, 'I think we're wasting our time here.'

Everyone looks at him, even Mary turning around.

Now he's standing up.

'I was never keen on protection duty anyway. Putting yourself at risk for people who were probably part of the problem.'

Catherine stares at him in astonishment and then starts to cry. Anne and Mary now looking at each other and then goes to comfort her mother.

Becket has to look away so they don't see the laughter in her eyes. Clever old bastard that he is.

'So, I don't know about you, but I'm off to see if I can get a decent pint of beer in this godforsaken place,' he continues and makes for the door.

Becket sighs and goes to follow him.

'Hey,' says Mary. ' You can't do that.'

Fletcher turns at the door.

'Just watch us, neither of us ever good at doing what we're told . . .'

Becket shakes her head.

'It was him, always led me astray . . . or taught me to look after myself.'

But now Catherine goes towards them.

'Please don't abandon us, I'll pay you whatever you want.'

Becket can't hold back a sneer.

'Do you think we do this for money?' she growls.

It's at this moment Ellie appears at the doorway.

'Couple of heavies on the wall looking at the house,' she whispers.

Becket's thinking if that's a ploy, it's smart, but then she sees her eyes and realises it's not.

She follows her out, while Fletcher ushers the family downstairs.

The two of them run quickly up the stairs and peep down at couple on the ramparts.

They could be American, one guy has a smart looking camera, while the other one is pointing further along the walls, but then two kids come running back, shouting at their 'fathers' who laugh and set off after them.

Becket sighs, then grins.

'That was clever,' she says.

Ellie blushes.

'No, I really thought they might be them.'

But then Becket whispers.

'Well, we'll use it to get them to do what I want. So you stay here.'

Ellie's okay with that, she doesn't like cellars.

So she pushes one of the abandoned armchairs up to the window, turns it round and kneels up on it, where she can see both ways.

The usual passage of desultory visitors doing the walls like it's a penance and looking forward to the pub or the café.

*   *   *

Otka's not sure what to do after Ellie disappeared.

She thinks they could help but being the people who have caused quite a lot of this trouble, she can understand why they're not keen.

The thing is they could do with the money from selling what they stole.

'But we don't know where he put them!' she says to herself out loud.

Xavi stares at her.

She glares at him.

He shrugs, he's only the catcher.

But he follows her as she stomps off in the same direction Ellie went.

She soon realises they won't catch up with her, lots of alternative routes available and the old town by the walls is a complete maze.

So, she turns round and sees Xavi coming towards her, following her like he always does. Sometimes it's annoying, especially if she's latching onto a likely guy to have some necessary sex, but mostly it's reassuring, knowing how strong and protective he can be.

But then she sees the two other guys.

They are so out of place, as one of them turns to pretend to be interested with what's over the wall, which she knows is very little, just humps of grass which cover the older fortifications.

She links her arm in Xavi's and pinches his thumb.

He frowns at her and then realises she's indicating the two men.

So she leads him towards them, apparently wondering what the two men are looking at.

They turn away and go back the way they came, which just confirms her intuition.

She takes out her phone and pretends to be taking a photo, until one of them looks round and he snaps him, puts him straight into her bad guys records and she's right: Teodor Vacarescu, wanted for various serious crimes in Europe and US.

Not good.

'What?' asks Xavi.

'Them,' she nods after the two guys who are now taking one of the steps off the wall and disappearing.

She resists the urge to look over after them straight away, while she texts the photos to Voudra and then tells Xavi to look over the wall.

He looks both ways and then shakes his head.

She goes now and looks herself, just in time to see a grey Mercedes sliding away.

*   *   *

'Sometimes in your life fortune favours you when you least expect it.'

Before what happens next Fletcher would have given anyone saying this a shake of his head or a sarcastic comment, but this is just what happens and it's the irritating teenager who finds it.

Probably because Anne was sulking and hated being told what not to do, she wanders off into the maze of rooms in the cellar and then feeling mischievous thinks she'll play hide and seek without telling anyone.

So . . . a cupboard in the corner of the room seems a likely hiding place.

She creeps in and closes the door.

She isn't afraid of the dark but puts her phone light on.

Whatever this cupboard was for it is empty now, as there are no shelves or anything else apart from a stack of old picture frames leaning against one side.

But then she sees what looks like a light switch and presses it.

Whatever she thought might happen is definitely not the wall to her left opening soundlessly.

She gasps but then shines the phone light through the gap to see steps going further down.

Her mother's voice in her head tells her not to, but that just urges on her on.

Downwards.

Her brain calculating where this could be going? But then remembering the house was on the walls or rather the front part of the house was, she can remember seeing the back yard below.

But then these steps are going lower than that?

And the air is colder.

Damper?

And now there's another door.

She fumbles with the handle and it does that awful scrunching noise you hear in horror movies.

Now a tunnel.

The sounds of small creatures scuttling.

Anne would be screaming now, terrified of mice never mind rats.

She points the phone down the tunnel. Cobwebs and a cobbled floor.

And a door.

Twelve paces. Cobbles slightly greasy.

A barred grille at eye level like in a prison.

She peers through and realises there was some natural light beyond.

She tries the handle.

It turns but the door won't open and then she sees the keyhole.

Feeling round the nearby walls she can't find another key and sighs.

Adventure over?

But then she can hear voices.

Can't make out what was being said. Two men she thinks. Not angry or loud, just a conversation . . . then they stop or leave the room.

Silence.

So, having nothing to try and pick the lock with, she has to retreat and tell the others what she's found.

*   *   *

RALPH

I'm sitting here in the dark wondering what this means?

Why?

If I am a ghost . . .

It does explain why everything is so strange.

A Protestant priest would tell me it was a Catholic lie to try to make me feel guilty, but then if I am a ghost then what did I do wrong? Does this mean only some people can see me?

And then how long is it since I became a ghost?

Can I go through walls as well as doors?

I look around and choose a piece of wall beside the doorway.

And slip through like a knife through butter!

Now outside I contemplate the graveyard.

Have they all become ghosts? Or is it just some people? Or do you have to be dead for a long time to become a ghost?

And how long are you a ghost? Forever?

So many questions . . . but no answers?

Looking round this graveyard there's no sign of any other ghosts ?

These gravestones are all eighteen and nineteen hundreds?

The one the girl was standing by is seventeen ninety-three.

Anyway this makes more sense, the more I look at them. If the oldest ones are over two hundred years after when I was alive, then this church was built long after I died and that castle over the way as well?

But Elizabeth's walls are still there . . . just as I remember them?

Although I'm not certain and it is still dark outside, I think I might risk running over to the gateway which I think is the Cowport and see what happens.

Well! That answers one question, which I hadn't asked.

Although I can go through walls that were built after I was alive, I can't go through the old walls . . . and although it didn't hurt, it was more real . . . to me?

So?
So what?
What can I do?
Is it just me?

Will I live forever?
And what year is it . . . here?
Now?

CHAPTER SEVENTEEN

It turns out that one of the guys Tomasz knows quite well.

'Simmo' was with him in the Crimea for a few months before Tomasz was captured. They'd had a couple of phone calls since he'd come home, but nothing else, so he is immediately suspicious.

But that didn't stop the welcoming handshakes and introductions to the other two guys, Jones and Grafter.

'Anyway,' says Simmo, 'the grapevine tells me you're under siege from some American gangster, who thinks you've kidnapped his wife and daughters.'

Tomasz frowns and then shrugs his shoulders, knowing the 'comrade grapevine' is always there.

'Yeh, well, I'll believe it when it happens . . . and we're well armed and ready, so . . .'

Simmo glances at the old lady and the woman he thinks must be his sister.

'Yeh . . . but . . .'

Tomasz smiles.

'There's a couple of others you haven't seen yet, but they're here,' and nods at Gill looking down from the sitting room window and then Walker coming along the balustrade, although he doesn't tell them to look up to the roof where he knows Imelda will be watching.

It's then Walker shades his eyes and stares at the guy introduced as Grafter.

He's quicker at recognition and raises his gun to point it at him.

'I think we know each other . . . don't we, Frank?

The guy freezes. He thinks of reaching inside his jacket but then realises there are another three or four guns pointing at him.

Half an hour later the three men have been stripped and searched, guns and phones confiscated and locked up in separate rooms in the cellars.

Walker's now on the phone calling for support saying that these three guys have been caught trying to break into the house.

An hour later it's all done and dusted. The three of them taken away by some tight-lipped military police, who Walker's superiors decided to co-opt, without much explanation, but it made everyone feel a bit safer that at last the authorities were beginning to see that this is a serious matter.

'Well,' he mutters, 'that's a surprise . . . apparently they'd be given a tip off by someone who said they were working for some American guy.'

Tomasz shrugs.

'That'll be the husband I suppose?'

Walker nods.

'I suppose so, but they said they didn't know whether he's in the UK yet but are on the lookout.'

Tomasz looks away.

'I wouldn't count on that, people like him have private jets and plenty of money to find a way past the usual procedures.'

Magda sighs.

But Helena laughs.

'That's the best bit of fun I've had for years,' she shouts, but then frowns.

'It's shame we didn't get the chance to 'persuade' them to tell us what they knew.'

Magda shakes her head.

'Mother! Really! I don't think the police would have approved of you pulling their nails out or sticking them in the freezer!'

Now everyone's laughing, releasing the tension.

Except for Imelda, who has finally come down from the roof.

'I don't think they were alone,' she says quietly and points across the valley.

'There was a car there shortly after they arrived and it's gone now.'

Everyone looks at where she was indicating, but as she said, nothing to see now.

Tomasz frowns.

'Well, let's just take a breath . . . and then back to positions.

This was done without a word spoken, although there were a few looks and glances checking out each other's faces.

Mostly hard and more determined.

*   *   *

URSULA

I was expecting that we would be going to stay with Sybil again, but Louisa just shakes her head and mutters something under her breath that I can't hear but assume is not very complimentary.

Eventually she pulls up in the middle of Berwick outside a rather posh hotel.

Ten minutes later we are 'ensconced' in a second-floor suite which has two bedrooms and two other rooms and the car has been put in the garage by a man in a green uniform.

What I wasn't expecting was that it has a sea view including the estuary.

And now we're sitting on a little balcony having drinks.

'This is better,' she announces and I can't help but agree, not daring to ask how much or for how long.

Now she's on the phone and I eventually gather it's Catherine she's talking to, so she does most of the listening, with only a few 'oh dears' and a few 'reallys'.

So by the time she ends the call I'm quite intrigued.

She sighs.

'Apparently, the youngest daughter, Anne, is being a bit of a problem, including just now reappearing from exploring a hidden tunnel in the house, which was very worrying, because they didn't know where she'd been.'

I shake my head, glad that I don't have to deal with teenagers.

But then I'm thinking that might be where the missing items might be stored, but Louisa's telling me it's not.

So . . . no further.

'It'll end badly' as my mother always said.

I look out the window.

The sky is blue and the estuary looks empty, so it must be low tide. No boats and the swathes of mud make me think that only small boats could get in even at high tide.

And then there's a heron, landing with that awkward but graceful way they have. A shuffling of wings into place and then still. Eyes down. Fish beware.

It's then that I realise I'm not worrying about my ghostly friends . . . although this heron may be a substitute, so I wave at it.

And then I realise Louisa's looking at me.

So I manage a suppressed giggle.

Louisa shakes her head.

We sit in silence watching the river.

Until she sighs.

'Actually I'm tired of all this . . . 'skulduggery,' she murmurs . . . what I really want is . . . a damn good f**k.'

I feel my eyes swell into saucers but I don't look at her, just hope it's not that immediate.

So now she's on the phone, swishing through her address book.

'Aha,' she growls, and presses a number.

By the time it's answered she has gone back into the bedroom.

The only thing I hear is a couple of darlings and then girlish laughter, but then a quieter conversation.

Two minutes go by and then she reappears, a wadge of notes in her hand which she pushes at me.

'Ursula, darling, be a love and 'eff-off' for a few hours, go for a walk on the Walls, get yourself a meal , whatever . . . I'll call when I've finished.'

So, five minutes later I'm out on the road, not knowing where I'm going.

*   *   *

Catherine thinks they should barricade the door to the passage, but Fletcher and Becket are both thinking it might be an alternative escape route.

So Fletcher tells Anne to show him the way and then Ellie finds a torch and goes with them.

Becket has suggested Catherine and Mary should see what they can rustle up for a meal, while she'll continue doing lookout.

Anne can't help being excited, but a frown from Ellie makes her calm down.

It doesn't take long to reach the locked door.

Ellie runs her hands all over the nearby walls, knowing that there's often loose bricks and dusty corners where keys get hidden, but there's nothing.

Fletcher had looked for some tools upstairs but couldn't find any, so they decide to figure out where it might come out by counting the steps back through the tunnel, which is obviously going to be outside, probably beyond the back yard.

202

Then they think they'll go out the back door and find that door is locked as well. But no key.

Ellie wants to climb up onto the wall, but Fletcher spots the nasty shards of glass embedded in the concrete on the top so they realise they'll have to go round to the back entrance.

But then find there isn't a back alley, because it backs onto another building's back garden . . . which is abandoned and overgrown with weeds and rubbish. So they go round to the road behind.

To find that house has been abandoned for a long time. Huge rusty padlocks on the door and glass shards on the top of all the walls.

They stare at the façade of what was probably a fine Georgian house, Ellie guesses.

'Not my period, but the big glass windows are a giveaway,' she murmurs.

Fletcher can't help but smile and ponders what his period might be. Post-war Clapham?

'So who will know?' he asks.

They both frown, and then both say 'Sybil' and laugh.

Ten minutes later they're having a coffee in her warm kitchen.

'Gosh,' she mutters, 'it must be twenty years since it's been left abandoned.'

'But haven't the council done something about it? It's a bit of an eyesore,' asks Fletcher, thinking what does he know about any council's ability to make someone tidy up? Make it safe?

Sybil shakes her head.

'There have been petitions. I've signed them, but . . .'

'But someone must own it?' he adds.

Sybil laughs.

'Ah, 'nail on the head there' detective . . . but no-one seems to know . . . or say if they do . . .'

Fletcher shrugs.

'But there were suspicions that Henry knew and even that he had somehow bought it and then couldn't find the money to repair it,' she murmurs, putting her finger on the side of her nose.

'So . . .' says Ellie impatiently. 'I think it's a ladder and a carpet over the glass,' and she sets off back to Henry's.
Even that is problem, because they can't find one, so back to Sybil who has one in her garage.

Ten minutes later Ellie has found her way in after freeing the rusty corrugated covers from a downstairs window and lifting it open just enough for a skinny young dancer like her to get through.
Now she's disappeared.
Fletcher waits apprehensively.
No more sounds or calls.
Another five minutes, he's getting worried.
He climbs the ladder and leans in though the gap.
A musty room with what he thinks are pieces of furniture covered with cloths or curtains. Dark paintings on the walls.
And then there's Ellie, with a sooty face and a cobwebs in her hair . . . but her eyes are gleaming.
'It's a treasure trove!' she gasps.

*   *   *

Catching a snap of the disappearing grey car only gave Otka a couple of the letters on the registration - MC.
So what next?
Infuriated she walks to the wall and leans on it.
It's too wide to see down the other side, but she knows the tunnel down to the estuary road is to her left.
The tide is in, which she doesn't think she's seen before, but thinks it's not as ugly as the usual expanses of mud, which makes her think of home and the Vltava.
She sighs.

But then she sees the car, slowly cruising out from under the wall.

She watches as it continues along obviously looking for something and then she realises they're found out about the sister.

How can she warn her?

Pulls out her phone. Puts in her name, hoping she has kept the same surname as Henry.

Gets a landline number.

Calls her.

She answers.

'Hi, it's Otka, we met the other day when we were seeing things on the cricket ground . . .'

There's a slight pause, but then a laugh.

'Oh yes, I remember and I've been doing some research for you and . . .'

But Otka interrupts her.

'Listen you need to get out your back door and come up onto the wall immediately, there's some bad guys who might harm you . . . I'll tell you more when I see you, we're just above the tunnel.'

'What?'

'They're working for the American husband and he might have figured out that you're Henry's sister and that you might know where he hides things.'

'What?' she says again.

'Please, just do what I say, they won't hesitate to hurt you to find out what they want to know.

Joan is still confused but agrees to come.

Five minutes later she's up on the wall having slipped up the steep wynd next to the children's playground.

Otka rushes up to meet her, puts her arms round her and hugs her like she was her own aunt.

But then she hustles her and her little dog along the lane and into a café.

It takes her some time to catch her breath, while Otka's on her phone to Xavi asking if the guys have come back.

'What?' she says and listens.

'Well, see where they go next?'

She cuts the call.

'Good news is that they just knocked on the door but didn't try to get in . . . but the bad news is that I don't think they'll give up.

Joan is dumbstruck, but then wipes a tear away.

'But where will I go?' she whispers.

Otka pauses for a second and then says: 'you'll have to stay with us, it's just round the corner from here.'

*   *   *

URSULA

In the end I find myself up on the wall.

It's getting dark and I'm thinking I might go to a restaurant after all. I counted the money and found she had unbelievably given me over a hundred pounds!

So, where should I go?

I don't know Berwick at all really and I've never been here in the evening, so I think I'll go down the next steps and see if I can find my way to the main street where I recall seeing lots of cafes and restaurants.

This part of the town seems to be the oldest, but then Louisa said it's only two hundred years old or so and therefore 'Georgian'?

They look expensive, even if they've probably had very expensive restorations.

But now here's a new estate looking rather out of place with its cream walls and cars in the little driveways.

And then I see him.

A strange fellow, walking oddly, but I don't think he's drunk, more likely disabled in some way.

And then he sees me.

Looks at me like he's seen a ghost.

Freezes.

Then runs away . . . well, limping a bit.

He gets to other side of a big building which looks abandoned and disappears.

I stand and stare.

Was that a monk's outfit he was wearing?

A long brown cloak . . . and sandals on his feet.

A beard? Long hair like a hippie.

I thought Ziggy said there were no Catholics here or any monasteries either.

Anyway I'm then aware that there's a woman getting out of car near me.

'Are you alright?' she asks.

I do a double take.

Of course, she's perfectly ordinary, about my age, but I'm a bit confused by what I've just seen.

'Er, yes,' I say, and then realise I'm shaking.

Five minutes later I'm sitting in her kitchen, while she makes me a cup of tea.

She's called Yvonne.

I told her what I saw.

She shakes her head.

'Well, he can't have got into the Governor's House, it's all locked up. They're trying to sell it but it's a listed building in a conservation area so a big problem.'

I sigh and decide not to tell her I can sometimes see things other people can't.

Then half an hour later we're sitting in a restaurant, which she insisted taking me to, because she'd been out all day and had decided to do that anyway and she hated eating alone.

So when Louisa sent me a text to say I could go back to the hotel, I called and primly told her I was in the middle of lovely meal with a new friend, Yvonne . . . and may be quite late and not to wait up for me!!

The silence before she cut the call was worth it.

*   *   *

RALPH

It's just dawned on me that I need to make my way to the Governor's House, so as it's getting dark I think I'll risk going up by the Cow Port and onto the walls again..

If I remember correctly it's just a few yards towards the estuary and there's a way down from there.

It takes longer than I thought and there are people with dogs. The people still don't seem to be bothered about me, but the dogs act a bit strange, although I've never trusted them since I was bitten when I was child.

So eventually I'm down to where I remember the governors house, where Sir Richard and his entourage would make merry, whilst the likes of me were being beaten for some minor misdemeanour or just because he didn't like your face.

Although since the Italian came most of his anger and foul language was directed at him, but mainly behind his back as in the end he's a sly coward.

But then I see the building!?

My word, it's grown enormous.

Much higher, more windows and many more rooms.

But . . . again? Where are the guards?

Lee was always afraid someone would try to kill him . . . mainly because he made so many enemies.

But then I realise there's a woman staring at me, so I run round the side and find a door I can get through . . . literally!

I'm inside!

But it's nothing like I remember and it's empty.

No guards, no servants, no people?

But then I realise why.

This building wasn't here when the walls were being built . . . otherwise I couldn't have come in through the door.

Well?

What next?

And could that woman really see me?

CHAPTER EIGHTEEN

URSULA

I come awake with a start.
Panic.
Where am I?
Then I remember.
We're in a hotel in Berwick.
Louisa's in the bed by the window.
I can see her hair on the pillow. Silvery grey now, but still very beautiful.
Then I remember where I was last night.
Coming back from Yvonne's house, creeping into the room, trying not to wake her.
But knocking the glass off the bedside table spoilt that.
She turned over but didn't lift her head.
I got into the bed as quietly as I could, knowing full well she was awake.

But now she's sitting up and getting out of the bed.
I keep my eyes shut.

I hear her going to the bathroom.
I'm really worried.
Is this the end of our friendship.

Now she's come back.
I don't look.
I hear her humming, which is worrying, I've never heard her do that before.

Sounds like she's dressing.
What can I do or say?
Silence?

I can't bear it.
I turn over and look at her.

To find she's standing looking at me.
With a smile on her face?

'So . . .' she says. 'what was he like?'
I'm bewildered, how can she know about the man in the street?
'Who?'
'Come on, you can tell me,' she says with what I think is a wink?!
I shake my head, but then realise she's thinking I was having the same activity as her last night, so I laugh.
'No . .. I met this woman.'
Louisa's eyes go big and she laughs.
'No,' I say again, trying not to laugh as well.
'It wasn't like that . . . I . . . had a funny turn . . . I saw a strange man on the street.'
Now she's making a face like I must be lying.
She shrugs.
'Whatever . . . but I hope he was better than mine . . . bloody men, can't keep it up.'
'No, I didn't go with the man, as I said he was weird, long straggly hair, dressed like a monk and sandals . . . I was rescued by this woman who lives nearby.'
Now she's frowning.
'What do you mean 'rescued'?'
I look away feeling stupid.
'Oh, you know, as I said he was . . . different somehow.'
'Alright, how different?'
I shrug.
'Like he was . . . 'medieval'.'
She looks at me.
'Sounds like an old hippie to me.'
I look away, she could be right.
'So, had you been drinking?' she asks.

I'm finding this really frustrating, so I shout.
'No, I hadn't been drinking and . . .' and I burst into tears.

Five minutes later we are sitting having coffees, which Louisa had ordered from room service.

She's interrogated me again and I was able to relate the event more calmly.

But then her mobile grumbles.

She picks it up and decides to take it.

Listens and her face goes very serious.

'So, you're all okay?' she asks.

She listens some more and then laughs.

'Good for them.'

Listens some more and then ends the call.

I look at her.

She goes to stand by the window.

'We've been attacked,' she eventually says very softly.

I can only stare.

'However, no-one got hurt except the four guys who tried to break in.'

I continue to stare, just now realising that she's talking about her house.

'Apparently they tried to get in through the back door, but Ziggy saw them coming and alerted the Polish girls and they 'dealt' with them.'

'Dealt with them?' I whisper.

'Two unconscious, one still screaming and the other jumped into the river and was washed away.'

She's now shaking her head.

'He says not to come back but find somewhere to disappear and tell Fletcher what's happened.'

So she's back on the phone.

Her explanation is curt and there doesn't seem to be any questions and she cuts the call.

Then she walks this way and that which is her thinking mode.

'Right,' she says, 'who and where is this woman who picked you up last night?'

I want to say she didn't pick me up, but the icy glare scotches any defence I might be thinking of, and I tell her.

'It's only a couple of streets away.'

'C'mon,' she orders and grabs her coat.

Five minutes later I'm knocking on Yvonne's door.

It opens and we're inside and I'm trying to tell her what's happened until Louisa takes over.

'We've been targeted by some very angry men who won't stop at anything to find us.'

*   *   *

Fletcher is getting overraught.

He and Becket are used to fighting against the odds, often against people who were supposed to be on their side.

But this situation is getting untenable.

He makes Ellie come back with him.

The others all stare at her.

She's still got the black face, cobwebs in her hair and two bright eyes, as if she cared?

But then she gets a message from Ziggy.

Her eyes go even bigger.

But then she sees Catherine's staring at her.

She grins and says it's a friend, but she can see Catherine is suspicious, so she goes to tell Fletcher and Becket.

'So,' murmurs Becket, 'I think we can assume he'll figure out where else we might be?'

Fletcher sighs.

'But he won't know about Henry's hideaway?' suggests Ellie.

Fletcher and Becket exchange doubtful looks.

'Well, has anyone got any better ideas?'

Headshakes all round.

'I think this means you need to go back into the other house and see if you can get back through the tunnel.'

But Ellie isn't so certain.

'The place is full of stuff . . . and we'd have the same problem: no key and no electricity. I suspect it's been turned off by the supplier.'

So they're all quiet.

But then she gets a message from Ziggy.

She listens, frowns and sighs.

'You sure about this?' she asks.

She listens again.

Ends the call.

Everyone's looking at her.

She shakes her head.

'Where are the house keys?' she asks.

Becket takes them out of her pocket and offers them to her.

She fingers them until she finds an old key, holds it up.

'You won't believe where this is for.'

Fletcher shakes his head, knowing they tried them unsuccessfully at the house behind.

'Go on then . . .'

*   *   *

Joan is getting very fidgety.

'I need to do my shopping, you know,' she mutters and then bursts into to tears.

Otka goes to give her a hug.

'Look, we're worried about you, there are some very bad people out there who think your brother hid some things they want.'

Joan stares at her.

'What sort of things? He only bought and sold old stuff. I don't know how he managed. Never did a day's work in his life.'

Otka had to stifle a gasp. Then decided not to tell her the 'big picture' just now.

214

'Well, I don't know, but some of the things he bought and sold could be quite expensive, I think.'

Joan frowns.

'You mean like the Lowry paintings?'

Otka nods.

'Yes, but some things even more . . .'

Joan's eyes go big.

'More?! Do you know how much my Lowrys are worth?'

Otka nods and smiles.

'I do, but . . .'

Joan sighs and looks out the window.

'So all this time he's being buying and selling things worth thousands?'

Otka nods again.

Joan shakes her head and pulls out her handkerchief again.

But then Otka's phone beeps and she sees it's Voudra, so she takes it over to the window.

She listens.

'So, ETA?'

She shakes her head.

'Okay, I'll tell the others.'

Ending the call she holds the phone to her chest and stares out at the estuary . . . wondering if she's had enough of all this excitement . . . after all they don't need the money anymore, what they've got in the bank accounts making them far more money on the stock market than climbing over walls and risking angry retribution from the folk they rob.

She sighs.

Turns round.

Joan's gone.

She dashes down the stairs, stares out at the carpark.

Rushes back up to find Xavi playing on his phone.

'She's gone!' she shouts.

He drops his phone and ducks whatever she's throwing at him, to see that she's just standing in the doorway . . . her face changing from anger to stone.

He doesn't even dare to pick up his phone or even whisper 'sorry'.

He waits.

But he can almost hear the frantic calculations she's making, knowing it will be the battle between flight or fight and that fight rarely wins.

'Okay,' she whispers.

'You go down to Joan's house and stake it out . . . the little shelter would be good . . . I'll go looking in the shops . . . we've got a couple of hours, but he might have sent on others who could be here sooner.'

He carefully finds his phone and slinks out, not saying a word.

Otka looks at her phone.

Bites her lip.

Not in her nature to put trust in anyone but her two lovers.

But in the end she realises the Ziggy guy will be on to this and so the others will know soon enough, so she calls Ellie.

Listens.

Eyes go big.

'Okay,' she whispers. 'See you there.'

*   *   *

RALPH

I've decided to go upstairs.

It's changed as much as the outside.

Lots of rooms, including a large one like an eating hall and then I find myself in a kitchen.

I know my place!

But there aren't any plates or knives or cooking pans and no open fireplace, no piles of wood, no dogs lying around, no busy servants . . . just a couple of sinks.

Otherwise empty
Abandoned?
Why?
Have the people in charge gone somewhere
else? More opulent?
I find some stairs.
I go up to the first floor and realise there's
another floor higher up.
I go to the top floor.
Where I can see the walls and the sea beyond.
A long wall going out to a tower, which I
don't remember.
No ships though?
I go through to another room where I can see
the town spread out before me.
But not as I remember it?
A huge tower a few streets away, much bigger
than I remember.
Not the church where I was earlier.
A couple of other towers.
And the town is much bigger.
Hundreds of rooftops.

How can this be?
It's enormous.
And where's the smoke?
How are folk keeping warm?

But then I'm not cold?
Not warm either?
Just empty.

Not even hungry?
Or thirsty.
So what do ghosts do?
Forever?

What's that?
Voices below.

*   *   *

Tomasz doesn't know what to do?

Which is a rare feeling for him.

It seems the focus of the attack has now drifted to Berwick, as the husband seems to have realised that his family aren't here anymore.

So should he take his cohort to assist the family there or just stay out of it and keep his own safe.

As usual it's his mother who makes the decision.

'You get yourself and your mates off to the seaside,' she tells him, 'we'll be alright here, he knows they've gone.'

He turns to look at her.

She looks like a woman in the Wild West. Hair loosely gathered but straggling across her face in the wind.

He grins.

But then looks at her sternly.

'Imelda and I will go, but I'll leave the others.'

She shrugs.

So half an hour later he's driving down the hill.

A glance at Imelda tells him she's not keen, although she didn't seem surprised when he told her the plan.

'Okay?' he murmurs.

She gives him a look.

The one that gives absolutely nothing away.

Back to staring out the windscreen.

It's only as he takes the back road to Berwick in Kelso, that she clears her throat.

'Where are we going?'

He frowns.

'I told you, Berwick . . . Ellie's a bit worried .'

'Yeh, but 'where' is it?'

He gives her a look, has she taken something?

'You know, the place with the walls.'

She shakes her head, but then frowns.

'Ah,' she murmurs, 'the creepy place.'

He sighs, thinking perhaps it is at night, all those empty buildings.

'Ghosts,' she mutters.

He laughs.

'Really? You believe in ghosts?'

She looks back at him.

'Of course . . .'

He doesn't laugh again.

But it's the place to go for ghosts, he's thinking.

Half an hour later he pulls up in the YHA car park.

Fingers his phone and waits for Ellie to respond.

'We're here,' he says.

He listens.

'I think so, not far from the back of Henry's.'

Listens again.

'Okay,' and starts the engine.

Two minutes later they can see Ellie waving at them and he pulls over and parks behind what he thinks must be the back of Henry's.

They get out. Tomasz and Ellie do kisses, but Imelda only offers a nod.

Instead of going up the wynd to the walls, Ellie beckons them towards a big building, which is all closed up.

Tomasz is shaking his head in disbelief.

It's the old Governor's House, been on the market for ages, but it's historical provenance would mean lots of obstructions to renovations.

Down to a door at the side and then up inside until they come out on the ground floor where the wife and the girls are sitting on the floor looking miserable.

'And next we're planning for the arrival,' Ellie announces, which gets a mixed response from them.

So at this point she gestures to him to come with her into another room, where he finds the two circus performers waiting.

*   *   *

Two black SUV Defenders and a silver Mercedes parked together at the edge of the motorway service area at Leeming Bar on the A1M south of Darlington.

Two drivers with hard eyes. Big shoulders.

A couple of clones in the back

Anyone thinking of staring changes their mind and carries on . . . quickly.

Not exactly undercover.

Inside the café there's a couple of other big guys, one sitting uncomfortably on one of the flimsy cafeteria chairs, while the other one is standing by the window, where he can see the Defenders.

If you'd seen them come in, eyes scouring the inhabitants, the doorways and the staff, you might have thought you had been transported into an American gangster film and quite a few people have decided that they'd better get going.

But in the queue for the refreshments there's a young woman, carrying tray with four mugs on it.

And finally a smaller man comes out of the toilets and goes to the table with an older man and the girl who's now distributing the mugs to him and this other man.

There doesn't seem to be any conversation.

The big man's constantly surveying the rest of the room.

The girl is looking at her phone.

The other man is listening to his.

The call ends.

He shrugs.

Says something to the big man and they drink their coffees and get up to go, followed by the man at the window.

The girl makes a face and follows, even though she hasn't drunk any of her coffee.

After they leave, the remaining customers and staff are shaking their heads and one or two now managing to smile, more out of relief than amusement.

One or two of them near the windows can see them get in the two SUVs and the Mercedes set off.

No-one voices it, but most of them thinking they're glad they're not the people at the end of those men's journey.

CHAPTER NINETEEN

Fletcher can't figure out whether he's drawn the short straw again or maybe the safest option.

He can just about remember the time he did what's now called 'witness protection' way up north in Scotland and that didn't have a happy ending.

But he finds himself hustling Catherine and her daughters along the wall and down an alley he now knows is called a 'wynd'.

In through a side door and into the YHA café, where he approaches the desk and tells them they're booked in, Ziggy having done the booking under his name.

Five minutes later he's down in the café having told the three of them to stay in their rooms on pain of death, whilst he sorts some drinks and food.

But then Louisa and Ursula both appear looking a bit shamefaced and a little bit scared, although Louisa quickly puts on a braver face and shakes her head.

'Fancy meeting you here,' she says sarcastically, but then thinking when would he have ever been in a YHA and wonders when he became a member?

Fletcher quickly puts them in the picture and they agree to book themselves in as well if Ziggy can do that.

Which of course he's already done.

Ursula is detailed to go and fetch their bags from the hotel.

But then he thinks he'd better get back up to the girls and their mother.

Mercifully they've stayed where he left them.

'So is the American father here?' demands Louisa, forgetting the woman and her girls are sitting in front of her, although the elder daughter now goes to the window.

Fletcher shrugs.

'I assume Ziggy's on their tail.'

*   *   *

Tomasz has now taken over another defensive situation in the old Governor's House, which as yet, Ziggy thinks is not known to the enemy.

He has confidence in Becket and Imelda and knows Ellie's the quickest thinker he's ever met, but not so sure about these two circus performers, who are the people who've caused this situation.

But now the tiny woman comes up to him.

Offers her hand.

He pauses then holds out his own hand and is astonished with strength of the grip.

He pretends to wince, but she just laughs and grips his hand harder.

'They are my life savers,' she says and turns to introduce Xavi, who has a gentler grip, but Tomasz knows that this guy catches people with them.

'So what's the plan,' she asks.

'Well, first I hope he won't find us, gives up and goes home, but from what I've heard that's not likely,' says Ellie.

'So . . ?' Otka asks again.

Tomasz shrugs.

'I think we can assume that he knows where Henry lived, so he'll go there first.'

She makes a face.

'He'll maybe search the house and find the tunnel.'

'But that's no use to him, because he's after the rubies and the glass.'

Ellie shrugs.

'There's plenty of other stuff in the house behind . . . maybe that might satisfy him.'

Again Tomasz makes a face.

'Nah, it's more than that, this is about someone having the audacity to steal from him.'

'But they're not 'his', they belong to Catherine's family.'

Tomasz shakes his head .

'Maybe that's why he married her . . .'

Ellie sighs.

'So why hadn't he sold them already?'

Tomasz stares at her, but then they both start laughing as it dawns on them.

'Because he didn't know!! Until Henry put them up for sale!'

Otka and Xavi look at each other.

'Hey, we didn't know they were so . . .'

She doesn't manage to find the word because Tomasz gets a call from Ziggy.

He listens, his eyes go wide and then he whispers okay and closes the call.

He's aware of the three pairs of eyes focussed on him.

He shakes his head.

'The father has been tracking his family through something the eldest daughter's been wearing.'

The trio are all now frowning.

'How?' demands Ellie.

'Ziggy only became aware of it when she went down the tunnel, because he lost contact when she was underground.'

Ellie is immediately on her phone to Fletcher.

She waits while he interrogates the girl.

'It's possible it's the bracelet he gave her for her last birthday?'

'Sounds right, I'll ask Ziggy.'

Ten minutes later after the girl was asked to go to the old bridge and back, Ziggy confirms it's the culprit.

'What should we do?' asks Ellie.

'You go get it and take it to Henry's house, put it in the bathroom. At the worst he'll maybe think she's left it there and it will give us heads up if he goes to find it.'

'But won't he know she's been to the YHA?'

Ziggy sighs.

'You got a better idea?'

Ellie pulls a face and then explains what he's said to the others.

But it's Louisa who makes the decision.

*   *   *

URSULA

I can't cope with all of this coming and going, which I suppose it's what 'dogsbodies' do, because now Louisa's decided we're going back to Sybil's house.

224

I'm staring at her wondering how that will be safer and how does she know Sybil will agree.

As if I'd asked this out loud she shakes her head.

'She won't be there, because she's gone to a wedding down south and I've got a key.'

Fletcher is also frowning.

'It's alright . . . they won't think we're there because we're going to lay a false trail,' she adds, looking at me.

I actually look round to see who's behind me thinking she can't possibly be me she means, but there's no-one there, just the rest of the café, hardly any customers in sight.

'Me?' I whisper.

'Yes you're going to take the bracelet to Tomasz in the Governor's House, where he and his little army are waiting.'

'But can't we just tell the police?' asks Fletcher.

She shakes her head.

'Did you hear what DI Walker said about the Berwick police.'

He frowns.

'What?'

But she's hustling me out.

So, off I go with the offending article in my bag.

Louisa says the easiest way, so I don't get lost, is to go straight up the wynd and follow the wall to the left till I get to the Main Guard and the Governor's house is just to the right.

Five minutes later I'm knocking on the front door, feeling bit stupid because it's obviously abandoned.

No reply.

But then Ellie appears to my right and I'm whisked through a side door, down some steps and inside.

Up three flights of stairs and into a huge empty space.

No, there's four people here: Tomasz sitting on a box, Imelda and the two circus people leaning on window ledges facing out to three different sides.

There's also another box with a kettle, a little camping stove and a clutter of mugs.

I have plenty of questions going round in my head, but don't get to ask them.

But then I remember what I've come for and pull the bracelet out of my pocket and offer it to Tomasz.

He handles it like it's going to bite him, but then places it on one of the boxes.

'You go back to Sybil's,' he smiles, like I'm a child doing an errand.

I do as I'm told, but thinking a tougher bunch you wouldn't want to be with, never mind fighting them.

I shiver all the way back along the Walls to Sybil's house, where the rest of them are already there.

*　　*　　*

Berwick, it turns out, hasn't got a hotel which rates high enough on Mr Hadley's 'must have' list, so the three vehicles pull up on the gravel of a large modern building west Berwick on the AI.

Hadley is the last to get out and it's obvious he's not happy, but then that's 'par for the course'.

His men are quickly taking the luggage inside, while the young woman is doing a pose like some Bronte heroine on the balcony, but then she starts to shiver so she gives up on the film and goes back to being the spoilt brat.

Too late, Hadley's gone inside.

She sighs and makes her way to the door.

Inside it's all polished wooden walls and other faux Scottish baronial tat, but she doesn't know that and just wonders where the pool might be.

This turns out to be another disappointment and so she has to settle for a long shower.

The unfortunate hired in staff are soon wishing they'd not taken the job and those who've never met any rich Americans before soon realised they didn't do polite.

But mercifully Hadley isn't here for a break, so they're all back in the SUVs and heading for the town.

It's a Monday, so the traffic is light and the streets aren't crowded, most people doing their shopping and the few visitors, having done the walls are now looking for a café or window shopping.

The driver of the first vehicle is following his sat nav which has told him where the best parking on the walls would be near to the winking signal he can see on his onboard screen.

The other two are finding it difficult in the narrow streets to keep up, but eventually they all arrive in the carpark.

Mr Hadley doesn't get out, but it becomes clear that the other two vehicles are ordered to go elsewhere and they disappear.

It seems a long wait, but eventually the man in the front passenger seat gets out, opens the back door and Mr Hadley steps down.

Dark glasses, obviously, but he then realises the sky is cloudy, so takes them off.

The other man points towards an old stone building with big gates like a prison .

Mr Hadley shrugs, indicating he's not interested in old stuff.

He also gives the church and its graveyard the same cursory glance, before asking 'where's the damn Walls?'

The other man points to what looks like a small tunnel, with a little pathway to the right side sloping gently up onto a gated path.

'There,' he says.

Mr Hadley shakes his head.

'Are you kidding me?' he asks.

The other man shrugs.

'I think it's a bigger drop on the other side,' he suggests.

Mr Hadley shakes his head and sets off.

Two minutes later they're through the tunnel and the second man is relieved to see that the walls are much higher on the outside.

'Okay, Don,' says Mr Hadley, 'but they're still not that high.'

'Don' gives a slight laugh.

'I think you'll realise the height difference from on top of the wall, sir.'

So they go back through the tunnel and up through the gate and then find themselves on the wall looking down towards some trees and beyond the sea.

Hadley puts his sunglasses back on.

'Okay, so where's Henry Grey's house?'
Don points to his right.
'Only a few hundred metres.'
Hadley puts his finger to his earpiece.
'Are you there yet?'
He listens.
'Okay. Go.'
He waits and then shades his eyes.

'Is that a golf course?'
'I think so, sir, yes,' as Don fingers his phone.
Hadley sighs.
'Magdalene Fields. Eighteen holes, six thousand yards.'
Hadley shrugs.
'Well, maybe, when we've finished the business.'
He gets a call.
'What?'
'No-one?'
He listens, his fists clenching.
Don softly shifts a step or two away, partly because of
imminent attack and also not wanting to know what's been said.

'Okay, so where has it moved to now?'

'How far?'

'Well, get after them.'

RALPH

I'm feeling trapped.
I go to the top of the stairs.
The voices are louder now.
Someone, deep voice, giving orders.
Got to be a soldier, barking like that.

I go down a bit further.

There are other voices.

Female.

Female soldiers??

I creep to a place where I can see down and see fast moving figures.

They don't look like soldiers, but then they're not from my time, so maybe that's changed.

Then I can see that there is a woman, who's too old to be a soldier and two girls as well. They seem to be very frightened.

But now I can see the man giving orders. He's not wearing any armour and he hasn't got a sword, just a strange black stick.

A young woman, blonde hair, and two other young people who are speaking in a foreign tongue to each other, but then in a strange English accent to the girl.

They all seem to have sticks of some sort and I think they're sort of getting ready for an attack.

Now the deep voice commands them to be silent.

They obey.

Are we being attacked?

Who by?

And then I become aware of someone behind me.

I turn to find a woman staring at me, dark hair, mean face, a long stick now pointing in my direction and it's then I recognise what they are . . . not sticks, but thin guns, her fingers on the trigger.

Now she's frowning and I understand she can't see me . . . but somehow aware of my presence?

I keep still.

She shakes her head and walks straight through me!

Which makes us both shiver!

I move slowly to the window, thinking I might go out, but then think I could just go through the floor . . . and why hasn't that happened already.

But then I glance out the window . . . where I can see the Walls.

And then I see him . . .

CHAPTER TWENTY

Hadley shakes his head and puts the phone in his breast pocket.

'Damn useless, I'm going to get myself some new security when this is over and we're back in civilisation again.'

But then he sees Don staring along the wall.

'What ya looking at, Don?' he demands.

But Don's speechless.

Hadley goes up to him and pulls him roughly round.

'What's the matter?' he shouts, but then looks where Don's pointing.

He shades his eyes.

Is it a woman limping towards him?

Angry face. Straggly hair.

Seems to be shouting, but he can't hear anything.

Is she shouting at him?

He backs away, some woman gone mad.

No it's man!

Long hair and a rough beard.

But he's upon him – 'through' him?

He can't believe what just happened.

It didn't hurt, just like a shadow crossing him.

He turns to look where he's gone but he's fallen down; now getting up, face burning with hatred.

Flesh burning away?

Hadley turns and staggers into a run.

Along the wall.

Doesn't know where it goes but he can see a gate.

He goes through it and turns to see if the maniac is still following him. Limping.

Is that his shoe falling off?

No it's his foot!

He turns and runs.

When did he last run anywhere?

He can see a man coming towards him with a dog, he rushes along to him, but the man gets out of his way, while the dog is barking at the apparition behind him.

He keeps going.

Turns again to see the monster is getting closer.

There's a cannon on the wall, but that's no use.

He keeps going, his lungs aching to stop.

Some steps, he goes up them, it's some sort of tower.

He turns at the top, but the creature's right there, reaching up to him, his hands like claws.

It grabs at him, the claws are icy, digging into his shoulder, the other one round his throat.

He can't breathe. He's being lifted up over the battlement.

He hears one rasping cry of his name, then he's falling, the creature falling with him, now screaming, no! Laughing?

He feels the crunching of his bones and blood surging everywhere and yet at the last moment he recognises the grinning face.

But .. ?

*　　　*　　　*

Don can't believe what he just witnessed?

This man, well, he thinks it was a man, long hair, a brown coat, no, a monk's 'habit'?

Just comes running 'through' the iron gates, no, really! Not jumping over them but running 'through' them . . . then he chases after Hadley past a cannon on the battlements, up onto a tower, a brief struggle and then both of them disappear over the wall.

He realises he's just standing there staring.

Did that just happen?

He looks at this other man who's having trouble with his dog.

He rushes up to him.

'Did you see that?' he demands.

The man frowns.

'You mean the mad man?'

Don nods.
'Yeh, but did you see the other guy attacking him?'
The man stares at him.
'What other guy?'
He shakes his head and strides away, dragging the dog with him.

Don backs away, but then thinks he must go and see what's happened to his boss.
Did he really go up that tower and disappear.
But then he sees that there's a crowd gathering by the tower. People looking over into the estuary.
People running. Others on their phones.
He doesn't know what to do.
Looks round and scuttles back along the walls.

*　　　*　　　*

URSULA

I decide to go along the Wall.
Go up past the small building, which is called the 'Main Guard', which oddly used to be the other side of the town, where a 'main gate' should be?
But then I see a fat man running towards me like he's being chased.
And he is!
By a skinny man with tangled hair, dark eye sockets, a long brown cloak, but as he goes past me I see that his feet are bare. No! More like claws.
I turn to watch as they run towards the little tower.
Up the steps.
They're fighting?
But before I or anyone else can do anything, they both disappear?
Over into the water?

Well, the tides in, are there rocks? Mud? I've never been up it to see.

What's that about?

My mother would be straight into her speech about the evil of drink, but I'm not sure. More like hatred.

But then I think I've seen that figure before.

Where?

Just in my dreams.

Or just two of those people in Lowry's paintings?

*   *   *

Ellie can't believe what she's just seen from the third floor.

Two men up on the Main Guard.

One of those stick people she keeps seeing. Thin, practically skeletal, rushing at another man.

Who is definitely not thin, overweight, in fact, and probably American, two cameras round his neck, silly hat, unnecessary expensive sunglasses. The stick man chases him back along the wall.

Is this a 'performance'?

Now they're climbing up onto the Coxon Tower? Fighting?

Then they both disappear over the battlements?

She's been up the tower and seen the drop.

If the tide was in there would be water but if not it would be rocks . . . and she doesn't know whether it's up or not.

But then she gets that hollow feeling that she knows that other people who are on the Walls may not have seen this and she'll have trouble convincing anyone of what she saw.

But . . . she did see it.

And now she's shivering.

*   *   *

Fletcher is at Sybil's.

The 'family' they're 'sitting' being sorted out by Louisa and Becket, so he's left it to them.

234

It's one of those houses where you daren't sit anywhere or know which room you're not supposed to be in.

So he's gone through into the front room, which is not a place where he thinks he can sit down on any of the elegant 'sofas' or equally uncomfortable antique looking chairs.

So he's standing at the window and sees the last few seconds of the event.

A fat man trying to run but stumbling and staggering up steps to the top of a tower.

Chased by another man who is so thin he's almost skeletal, with only one foot, the other limb ending in a stump . . . but no blood?

He's clothed in what looks like a monks outfit, but even that's in shreds and falling away as he clambers up.

Then they're tangled in a fight, which is incredible because as the thin man gradually loses his clothes and apparently his limbs, he's somehow able to force the fat man over the wall and they both disappear.

Did that actually happen?

He goes out into the hall, finds a key and opens the door.

But he's too late.

A gaggle of folk are scrabbling about on the tower, shouting and leaning over the wall, pointing down at the river.

He hasn't been up this tower but he's been to see the cannon further along and saw that the estuary is really wide there and often it's just mud and ribs of rocks unless the tide is in when it's covered with swirling water.

But now a police officer has arrived and tries to get through the throng, while calling for help on his phone.

*   *   *

RALPH

I can't believe it!
It's him.

235

Sir Richard Lee.

Just standing there looking out to sea.

Next to him some minion I've never seen before.

Without thinking I find myself 'flying' down to the wall.

I rush towards him.

He sees me.

Recognises me?

He's backing away.

My foot hurts.

I'm limping but I can still run.

'Through' the gate.

But now there's a man with a dog, which starts barking at me?

Lee has somehow got past me; I turn round and chase after him.

He's still as fat as I remember him, so I know I can catch him.

He stumbles past a big cannon and makes his way to a tower I don't recognise, but it's on the old wall.

I catch up with him as he reaches the top.

I grab at him.

He's screaming.

I get him up onto the wall . . . and somehow find the strength to force him over.

Now I'm just floating through the air, as he falls onto the rocks below.

He crashes onto a big sharp rock.

Blood spurts from his head and his limbs are all mangled up and juddering.

I rush down to him.

Go right up to his face.

His eyes are open.

He knows who I am.

He tries to scream but I push him in to the water.

But now I'm feeling faint.

My body dissolving into the air and the water.

A brief cold sensation.

Darkness comes.

At last.

CHAPTER TWENTY ONE

The police get a number of calls and as it happens there's quite a few of them at the station today, so it's only five minutes or so before they're cordoning off the tower and questioning people in the crowd.

Then the fire brigade arrives and ropes and ladders are put down to where a body is spreadeagled on the rocks.

But then it soon becomes apparent that numerous people say they saw two people fighting, so Coastguard are called and a couple of boats come skimming across the estuary and then start quartering the water looking for the other body.

One body is eventually taken away to be examined.

The police manage to close off a section of the wall and continue to search the area for any significant evidence.

But the breakthrough comes when they find a man sitting by the cannon further along.

He can't stop shivering and he seems a bit deranged.

They take him to the police station and he's seen by a doctor, who tells them that he's physically fine, but obviously in a state of shock.

So after wrapping him in a blanket, a cup of tea and some gentle encouragement from PC Yvonne Johnson, she eventually gets him to talk.

'Did you see what happened?' she asks.

He nods and starts to shiver again.

She waits.

'Did you know either of them.'

He nods and looks at her, with staring eyes.

She waits.

'He's my boss,' he whispers and then shudders.

She nods.

'Can you tell me his name?'

He nods back.

'Mister Hadley.'

She smiles.

'First name?'

He frowns, like he's forgotten or doesn't know, but then it comes back to him.

'Richard . . . although very few people call him that, he's just 'Sir' or 'Mister Hadley'.

She nods again.

'So you work for him?'

He sighs and looks away, but she gauges he's recovering a bit.

'Not an easy man, I'm guessing,' she chances.

He looks at her, shakes his head and then away again.

She waits.

'No, he wasn't,' he whispers.

She thinks maybe leave that line of questioning and asks something a bit more mundane.

'So were you here for work today?'

At first he seems to be about to say something but then frowns.

'I don't think you could call it work,' he mutters.

She waits, giving him an inquisitive look.

He puts his head in his hands.

But then shakes his head.

'I'll need protection,' he whispers.

'Protection? Why?' she asks.

But then her sergeant appears and gestures to her to leave him.

*   *   *

The local police don't get much warning and the operation is over before they can do anything about it.

The two SUVs are surrounded and the men offer no resistance.

They are shuffled into a couple of unmarked vans, which then drive off at speed, with flashing lights and horns blaring.

There wasn't time for any reporters to arrive except the local guy who's been told to keep out of it.

So an hour later it's as if it hasn't happened, although the few witnesses interviewed weren't able to provide much information either, just snapshots of the two men fighting . . . just one man running up the steps and climbing over the wall.

So now everyone's gathered in Sybil's house.

Catherine and the girls are bemused by what's happened.

Ellie and Fletcher give their versions, but nothing makes sense other than a man was chased up the tower and forced over the wall by a frail looking guy who somehow found the strength to do it.

And then they realise that Otka and Xavi have disappeared.

And now there's a knock at the door.

Becket goes to open it.

A man and a woman.

She recognises 'men in black' when she sees them, even if occasionally they're female.

Now everyone's in Sybil's dining room where there's enough chairs for them all to sit.

Fletcher introduces everyone and then suggests he'll give them his story. So he takes them into the front room where he witnessed the event.

Then it's Ellie's turn..

'Not sure what I saw,' she whispers.

The lead detective, DI Grant, waits.

'The man with the cameras was standing just the other side of the gate, then he was chased by this other man along the wall and they went up the tower and the second man pushed the other man over and fell with him . . .'

'Can you describe the assailant?'

She shrugs.

'Very thin, long hair like a tramp, limping . . . almost . . floating . . .'

'Floating?' asks Grant.

Ellie shrugs, she wants to tell him she thinks he was a ghost, but . . .

Grant waits.

'Well, he was very thin and . . . only one foot.'

Grant looks at her.

'Really? But how could he have managed to push the other man over?'

She sighs.

'Anger!? Madness? I don't know but that's what happened.'

He looks away.

'Did either of them speak.'

She frowns.

'I don't think so.'

He takes her back into the other room.

'I don't mean to disbelieve either of you, but . . . had you been drinking?'

Fletcher laughs, but then shakes his head.

'I've had a stiff whisky just now, but . . . that's what I saw.'

Grant can't help looking at Ellie.

She shakes her head.

'I don't drink . . . but . . . I have seen ghosts before.'

Now Grant can't help but look back at his sergeant, but she's just staring at the young woman.

Then he gets a call.

'I've got to take this,' he says and goes out into the corridor, nodding to his sidekick, who casts a schoolmistress's eye over the 'suspects'.

They can hear his voice, but it's only intermittent.

The sergeant is frowning, although she can't hear either.

He comes back.

He hesitates, glances at his sergeant, who's as curious as everyone else.

'Right,' he says. 'We'll go for now, but I must ask you all to stay here whilst we investigate.'

Louisa gives him a stern look.

'I'll make sure they don't go anywhere Inspector; you have my word as a magistrate.'

*   *   *

As soon as the officers are gone, Fletcher's asking where Otka and Xavi have gone.

'They were in the Governor's House with us,' says Tomasz.

Imelda shakes her head but doesn't say anything.

'They probably don't want to be found by the police,' rasps Becket, who never trusted them.

'My money is on they saw their chance and they'll have pocketed something and disappeared,' she adds.

Fletcher shrugs.

No-one has any better suggestions.

But now Ellie is staring at Catherine, which would make anyone uneasy.

Catherine frowns and looks back at her.

'You may think I was stupid to let him 'charm' me, but I soon knew what I'd done . . . he was a monster, so I'm not grieving for him,' she says in a wavery voice.

Mary puts her arm round her.

'We all fell for it, it wasn't just you, mum,' she says and gives Becket a look.

Becket looks away.

The room goes silent.

URSULA

But now Ellie is looking at a photograph on the wall.
She frowns and goes up close to look at it.
It's a group of scouts, smaller ones cross-legged on the grass, older men and one woman sitting on chairs and then older boys behind.
But it's the building behind them that's interesting her.
'Where's that?' she asks, thinking she has seen it somewhere.
Louisa comes to look at it.
'Oh, that's Sybil's husband, he and Henry met there. I think they both ended up being honorary members when they grew up.'
She pushes her glasses onto her head and scrutinises it.
'Yes, there he is and there's Henry,' as she points at two of the men sitting down.
None of the rest of us have ever met Henry, so we have to take her word for that.
'But where was this scout hut?' mutters Ellie.
'Oh,' says Louisa, 'it's just out the back . . . it's still there and I think Henry is still . . .'
But then she stops.
'He'll have a key!'

Ellie and Louisa look at each other and laugh, but then Ellie remembers they can't go to Henry's house, there'll still be police guarding it.
We're all bewildered until Fletcher gets it.
'That's where he's hidden the stolen goods!'
So now Louisa's on the phone to Sybil.
Then she's in the kitchen finding a couple of keys at the back of a drawer.

Five minutes later the whole gaggle of us are in the scout hut opening and closing drawers and cupboards, but inevitably it's Ellie who screams and holds up a handful of glistening red stones in the air!

But then she looks at Catherine and smiling offers them to her.

And Catherine just weeps as she holds the necklace in her hands and I'm thinking she's just holding a necklace of rubies which was worn by Mary, Queen of Scots . . . who's neck was severed by an axe . . . well, at the third try, so Ellie told me.

And it doesn't take long to find the Elizabethan glasses, carefully filed behind some ordinary glasses in a different cupboard.

'Just think,' says Catherine, 'the idea of a gaggle of boy scouts having their orange juice and not knowing how precious they are!'

But next we have to tell the police, so we go back to Sybil's and Caroline makes the call.

*   *   *

The rest of the day passes in a procession of visits from different police officers and 'important' people asking a variety of questions about the man chasing the other man and him falling off the tower and others wanting to know how they found the treasure.

So it's going dark when Ellie wants to go back out onto the walls.

Fletcher is doubtful, but then realises there is street lighting and the tower is cordoned off.

She goes to stand next to the cannon – Crimean War definitely not her period – but it gives her a good sight of where the two men fell.

Nothing to see now.

The fire brigade had to be pretty quick to rescue Hadley's body, but too late to find the other man, who seemed to have floated away.

The tide has been out and now coming back, water lapping the base of the tower.

So she thinks maybe he might be washed further up the estuary, rather than out to sea.

But, hey, what does she know about the tides here?

'Nada' she whispers.

'What?' asks Fletcher.

'Nothing,' she murmurs, 'just wondering where the other body might be?'

He shrugs, looking at the swirling water reflecting the lights, which is quite eerie.

He shivers.

'Getting cold,' he says, looking at Ellie who's only wearing a T-shirt and tattered jeans.

They set off back to Sybil's, but at the last minute she goes back to the wall.

'Did you hear that?'

Fletcher looks back at her.

'What?'

She shudders.

'Like whispering.'

He shakes his head.

'Come on you, you'll be seeing ghosts again.'

She shivers again, but he grabs her by the arm and frogmarches her down to the house.

But she's still thinking about what she saw, until the synapses connect.

She stops him at the door.

'Did I hear right that Catherine's husband's surname is 'Hadley'?'

Fetcher frowns.

'Yeh?'

'And his first name is Richard?'

He shrugs.

'Yeh?'

She can't help but shake her head.

'Like 'rich'-'had'-'lee'?'

He still doesn't get it.

She shakes her head again.

'I told you; he's got the same name as the man who built the walls!!' she cries.

Ellie can't stop herself from whooping and screaming and then she has to ransack Sybil's bookcases until she finds the words that convince them that Sir Richard Lee built the walls for Elizabeth the First in the 1550s. and this horrid American had the same name.

But she can't get them to be as astounded as she is and in the end she realises she'll just have to keep it to herself, but then she contacts Ziggy, who, of course, has seen everything and confirms she's right.

*   *   *

Otka looks out of the window as the plane climbs steeply from the runway.

Last minute dash and taking whatever got them out of the country. Paris being a bonus.

She shivers as the flashback takes her to the window in the abandoned house.

Seeing Lee's face she recognised from the photos she'd seen when Voudra was researching him. Standing there in the middle of the Wall, other people having to go round him. Typical American indifference to ordinary people, but then this weird man appears and chases him up a tower and both of them falling into the river.

She'd gone straight to exit mode.

A train to Newcastle.

Taxi to the airport.

Hardly a word spoken between them.

Now she opens her bag.

Pulls out the two watches.

She'd slipped them into her pocket, while they were at Sybil's.

She assumed they must have belonged to her husband and gathering dust for all that time.

And she probably doesn't know how expensive they are.

But at least it will cover their fares there and back.

Xavi's taken something to get him through the flight.

Voudra tried to sound cross, but she knows she was relieved they got out unscathed.

And there's a story to tell.

'The fat American being chased over the wall by a vagrant.'

*   *   *

Quite a lot of people like walking on the walls in the dark and recently the council had a gang of men implant small lights beside the paths in places where people might fall.

So there's plenty of people tonight, especially those who've heard about the incident and want to see the place where it happened, although there's nothing to see except the police cordons.

And even when some lads who've had a lot to drink ,climb over them and go up on the tower, they still can't see anything.

Eventually there's no one there.

Just the tide on the turn.

The waves finding it harder to get the better of the river.

But then the battle turns and the river surges forwards.

The sea retreats back into its home.

Taking whatever its got in its tentacles.

*   *   *

RALPH

I'm floating in the water.

The sea.

It's dark.

But now I can see white shapes floating with me.

One of them nudges into me.

A swan.

Its neck hovering above me.

It reaches down and pecks at me.

Pulls at my arm.

Another one comes the other side. Then there are lots of them.

Pecking away.

It doesn't hurt me.

One of them makes a strange honking sound.

More of them arrive.

There's a bit of squabbling, but I'm not much of a meal.

Now they've stopped pecking but they're still floating with me.

It's then that the sound comes.

Not easy to hear it above the waves and the rippling of the currents.

A shushing noise.
Like people with fingers to their lips.
Wanting you to listen.
Not talking.
Because, if you listen very hard, you
can hear voices.
Maybe singing.
No . . . more like talking?
Crying?
Swooning?
A crowd.
Of indeterminate voices and words
      a shushing
        susurration . . . .
           of . . . .
              ghosts . . . .

NOTES

Sir Richard Lee was partly responsible for the building of the Elizabethan Walls in the 16th century. He was a frequent litigant with numerous people regarding property and financial matters. He died without a male heir.

People began to emigrate to the Americas in Elizabeth's reign.

LEE, Sir Richard (1501/2-75), of Sopwell, Herts. | History of Parliament Online

The walls were constantly repaired even after the union of England and Scotland in 1603, including against French invasion in the late eighteenth century.

The current building called the Governor's House is Georgian, dating from early 18th Century THE GOVERNOR'S HOUSE, Berwick-upon-Tweed - 1370859 | Historic England and is likely to be built on the site of the Elizabethan Governor's House.

Norham Castle is situated about ten miles from Berwick along the Tweed, but currently closed for renovations.

History of Norham Castle | English Heritage (english-heritage.org.uk)

There are four bridges over the Tweed at Berwick.
The old bridge was built after Elizabeth's reign in 1624 and the 400th celebrations are being held this year.

Berwick Bridge - Wikipedia

The railway bridge is a Grade I listed Stevenson bridge.

Royal Border Bridge In Berwick Upon Tweed - Fabulous North

LS Lowry regularly visited Berwick all his life and known for his thin 'stick people'.

Lowry Trail - Berwick Preservation Trust
LS LOWRY EXHIBITION AT THE GRANARY MAY- OCT 2024

ACKNOWLEDGMENTS

Linda Bankier - Archivist at Berwick Library.

Derek Sharman - Berwick local historian & guide.

Sandra Gann & Anne Humphrey
for local knowledge and encouragement.

Keith Smith
Palace Green Scouts.

and

The 'TEAM' at the GRANARY YHA café.

Goo